You Have Given Me a Country

Neela Vaswani

Sarabande  Books

LOUISVILLE, KENTUCKY

Managing Editor
Sarabande Books, Inc.
2234 Dundee Road, Suite 200
Louisville, KY 40205

Library of Congress Cataloging-in-Publication Data

Vaswani, Neela, 1974–
You have given me a country / by Neela Vaswani.—1st ed.
    p. cm.
  ISBN 978-1-932511-82-6 (pbk. : alk. paper)
  1. Vaswani, Neela, 1974—Family. 2. East Indian Americans—Biography.
  3. East Indian Americans—Fiction. 4. Racially mixed people—Biography.
  5. Racially mixed people—Fiction. 6. Biculturalism. I. Title.
  PS3622.A86Z46 2010
  813'.6—dc22
  [B]
                              2009041821

ISBN-13: 978-1-932511-82-6

Cover design by Ami Jontz.
Text interior by Kirkby Gann Tittle.

Manufactured in Canada.

This book is printed on acid-free paper.

Sarabande Books is a nonprofit literary organization.

The Kentucky Arts Council, the state arts agency, supports Sarabande Books with state tax dollars and federal funding from the National Endowment for the Arts.

This project is supported in part by an award from The National Endowment for the Arts.

For Holter

Sage Narada challenges the divine sons of Shiva and Parvati:
"The first to circle the world thrice eats this, the sweetest mango."

Skanda mounts his peacock, flies three times around the world
Wingbeats swift like time and death, three times around the world.

Dismounts, demands the prize. "Nah," says Narada. "Your brother won."
While Skanda flew, Ganesh walked, palms pressed together, three times
around his parents.

What follows is real, and imagined.

YOU HAVE GIVEN ME A COUNTRY

December 25, 1980

This place; that place. You have to stand someplace. I pledge allegiance to the in-between.

I am six. My mother: thirty-two. It is our first visit to India, my father's country. On Christmas Day, we leave New York with our rolling suitcase, my father delighted that the ancient invention of the wheel still improves human life in new ways. "Such elegant machinery," he says, "Revolutionary. One hundred percent guaranteed." We have never before owned a suitcase on wheels.

Half an hour before the plane lands, my mother walks me to the bathroom and I change from a tracksuit to a salwar kameez of green paisley. I believe if I stand too close to the toilet I will be sucked out into the clouds. My mother changes to a pink salwar kameez stitched with rows of black beads. She pats the beads gently, then laughs, "Christ Almighty, it's like I'm sewn into a rosary. Walk a mile in a man's shoes. . . ." She raises a finger as she speaks so I know it is a lesson.

At Dum Dum Airport, Calcutta, the hot air is fluffy with mosquitoes that hover but do not bite. My mother gives me a candy cane wrapped

3

in plastic. "Little bit of Christmas," she says. The air blooms with zinnia-colored saris and flashes of gold. Doors, windows, flung open to the long dark hem of horizon, the sun rising like a bloody egg. A woman sweeps the floor with a broom of sticks, moving in a squat like a crab. Two policemen with black guns lean against a wall. I tighten my fingers around my father's pant leg. He looks down at me and says, "Calcutta," his loss, joy, mingled.

Just past the baggage claim, the Vaswani-Jhangiani clan stands shoulder to shoulder. My father waves and nineteen hands wave back. "Oh, she looks just like Dadi, oh, so sweet, *chhoti babi, Arrey,* why are you cribbing? Let me get closer, *guee a me sura. Arrey,* so fair, *keeyañ ah eeñ, beri hi paar.*"

I am comforted by the faces and bodies like mine. The stories come true. Everyone speaks like my father, a jumble of Sindhi, Hindi, English. My father meets the children born in his absence. They shake his hand solemnly and call him Uncle. The women study my mother's blue eyes, the vivid white streak in her reddish-brown hair. Someone says, "Like Indira Gandhi." My mother replies, "White hair. Curse of the Irish."

I unwrap the candy cane. It sticks to my hand. Minty sweetness, distant Christmas. I suck the red stripes into white while my parents dole out bottles of duty free Johnny Walker Black Label and Revlon lipsticks that sweat in the heat. My cousins are suspicious of the Michael Jackson poster rolled in a tube. "Counterfeit," they whisper.

I lie on my back on top of the wheeled suitcase and play my favorite game: Unfocus Your Eyes. Everything goes indistinct, indefinable. No man, no woman, no table, no chair. The world, a soft blur. Swashes of color, flickering shapes.

I snap back to focus.

A pigeon. Inside the airport, flapping near the rafters. In the Indian comics I read, there are peacocks, crows, sparrows, hawks. But no pigeons. I think it is an American bird. This one must have flown from New York to Calcutta, like me. I love pigeons. Their orange eyes and pink feet. Their necks, iridescent purple and green, mysterious as an oil slick in a parking lot.

4

A woman with my father's face leans over me. "I am Gagi Auntie. What are you looking at, *beti?*"

I point. She says, "Ah. *Kabootar.*"

The pigeon, so universal, it has a name everywhere. Not American. Not Indian. Just pigeon. It flies, loyal to itself. Citizen of the air, waving the flags of its two grey wings.

"Come," my aunt says, reaching down to lift me off the wheeled suitcase, "*Chhalo*, it is time for home."

I link my arms around her neck, lean my face against her shoulder. Feel a pin hidden under a fold of her sari. I shift my nose. Through the fabric, I smell the pin, like an old nickel at the bottom of my grandfather Kent's change purse. I think of him alone in America. He loves pigeons, too. He says they are fattest outside the library because readers are generous. He says they always find their way home.

At Dum Dum Airport, Calcutta, just arrived, I feel the grief of leaving. Everything is a temporary reunion. It will be painful to leave my family in India, as it was painful to leave my grandfather and America. No matter where I am, I will think of lives being lived across the world. India, America. This place, that place. You have to stand someplace.

My lips harden to beak; my fingers melt to the softness of feathers. I look down at the world: a soft blur. Always in-between. And, in-between, home.

THIS PLACE, THAT PLACE

On April 1, 1973, my mother married in Elkton, Maryland, a brackish wind off the Susquehanna tweaking her violet sari as she stood on the front steps of City Hall signing the license against my father's proffered back, her signature slanted where the pen bumped over his spine. No church, no priest. No family present. In marrying an Indian citizen, in later bearing a mixed baby, she broke her religion. Broke from the long line of close-knit Irish-Catholic Sullivans. Broke the extant anti-miscegenation law in Maryland's constitution, struck down six years earlier but still in the pages and memorized by law students.

Two years before my parents married, my father had flown into JFK with his forehead pressed against the slick window of the plane. Forty-four dollars, an H1 work visa, and a photocopy of his medical degree, stuffed in the right front pocket of his grey polyester pants. He was alone with one tiny suitcase. As the plane turned south, he saw the green arm of the Statue of Liberty, a speck in the harbor, felt the same crash of wonder my great-grandmother, Catherine Sullivan, felt when she saw that forearm in 1897 from the deck of a coffin ship bound for Ellis Island from Dingle Bay. She had noted its thickness: an arm capable of bearing harvests, children, sorrow. It was the bulk of the arm, the hard beauty of the woman's face that made my great-grandmother believe in America. She did not believe in an endless supply of butter. She did not believe that anything in life could be easy or free. Nor did my father. He stared at the foreign skyline and whistled a bit of Beethoven's Symphony No. 7 for courage, his cheeks sucking in and out like slim bagpipes.

—∞—

To my father, nationality was fickle, unreliable. He was born in the province of Sindh, British India, in 1945. By his second birthday, Sindh was in Pakistan. Sindh had not moved, but it changed countries. This fact, this dark absurdity, impressed itself upon my father.

On August 15, 1947, the newly independent nations of India and Pakistan were carved out of what had been British India. Partition made one country into two, segregated by religion. At the stroke of midnight, the Radcliffe Line went into effect and the country of India cracked.

Although the split was expected, the territorial parameters were not revealed in advance. The redrawn borders divided the states of Bengal and Punjab, and evicted the state of Sindh from India. Jammu and Kashmir were contested and remain so to this day. Fourteen million human beings were uprooted, relocated, rendered homeless and landless. Muslims in India fled to Pakistan; Hindus, Sikhs, etc. in Pakistan fled to India. They left behind everything and passed each other, going in either direction. It was a crisis of category and identity, and one of the largest migrations in human history. The region drowned in riots, reciprocal violence, and revenge killings. Trainloads of mutilated and burned corpses pulled into stations on both sides. New hatreds, permanent losses, lethal suspicions. Up to 1.5 million people were murdered, and at least 100,000 women— Sikh, Muslim, Hindu, alike—were raped and abducted. The nations of India and Pakistan steeped in grief from the moment their borders appeared on paper—an arbitrary line drawn by an English lawyer who at least had the decency to decline his fee of 40,000 rupees when he realized the damage done.

My father's first memory is of my grandfather explaining the word *partition* in English. He slapped his open palm against a wall and said, "This separates one side from the other." The wall my grandfather slapped was in Bombay. Neither he nor my father ever returned to Sindh or the city of Hyderabad or the house on Vaswani Street, named for the eight generations who had lived and died there before them.

—⁓—

The Vaswanis fled Sindh with only the jewelry on the women and a doctor bag. Sindhis were both Hindu and Muslim and had always lived side by side in peace, but the sudden influx of refugee Muslims from India bloated the province, inflamed tensions, and forced Hindus to flee. It was unexpected and crushing.

My grandfather left a patient's house, vials of blood clicking in the bag squeezed against his chest. He ran from a back alley into a street hung with drying green and yellow *dupattas*. Swept forward by the surge of people. On a doorstep, a dead woman, severed arms in her lap. A standing child, screaming. The library on fire. Choking smoke of murdered words. The head of an unconverted cousin in the gutter, braid undone, long hair flowing. Her chin, just like his mother's, exactly.

My grandfather ran home using shortcuts he never knew existed. By instinct, by necessity. When he found his family huddled together on Vaswani Street in front of the house and the peepul tree, he counted them. Over and over again. *Hiku, ba, tey, chaar.* One, two, three, four. Sita, Gagi, Chandru, Ashok. The howls of abandoned dogs shook the neighborhood. He stepped in the street, took a rope from the mango seller's tipped-over wagon. Flies, cows, monkeys, scorpions, fighting over bruised fruit. He thought of the fragile bones in the human wrist. Tied the forearms of his wife, daughter, eldest son to his own. He picked up his youngest, my father. Said in the boy's ear, "Don't let go of me."

They used two necklaces to pay and pushed onto a train going south. The bleeding conductor said the previous train had been hijacked. Set afire. Barred windows. All the people burned.

The train crept forward. Desert air lashed the bars. Land blurred by. At every lurch, waiting for the stink of gasoline, heat of flame. They wept

11

on the shoulders of strangers. Fought the sway and lull, an offensive balm. They slept standing up, leaning into each other, then awakened as if slapped, certain they had forgotten something. Someone. Sand slashing. Stinging cheeks. Sun baking the train's metal skin. Sweat. Wet as swimmers. No shadows in space tight with bodies. Fear sudden, mysterious as mold. They slept then awakened. Each time, strangers' faces, more familiar. Lip, nose, ear, braid, bangle.

When my grandmother took the children to the toilet, they bumped against her legs and clung to the blue *paloo* drawn tight over her head. Their first train ride. She anchored herself, held their waists. One by one. Kept them steady above the squatter. She stared through the hole to the ground speeding by. Wondered which country they were in. The wheels of the train banged out the question. India? Pakistan? India? Pakistan?

A total and complete loss, like the disappearance of the sun. All that remained of the land was the dirt of Sindh on the soles of their shoes. Somewhere around Thana, my grandfather said, "Stick out your feet," and scraped that Sindhi earth from his own shoes and the shoes of his sons, daughter, wife. He collected the soil in a scrap of newspaper that he folded into a funnel then shook into an empty vial. When my father's stomach gnawed, he shed thin, dehydrated tears, and my grandmother dangled the doctor bag from her hand so it swung back and forth, playful. "Here, here, take it." Her voice a croak.

Fifty-three hours later, they arrived in Bombay, five of fourteen million refugees. Before the train pulled into Churchgate, my grandfather tied the family back together with the mango seller's rope. Forearm to forearm. Picked up my father. Said in his ear, "Don't let go of me."

They were put on another train to Kalyan Camp, sixty miles from Bombay. Concrete barracks built by the British to contain Italian WWII prisoners. Each family quarter defined by a hanging grain sack. A water tap here and there. No toilets. The young, anguished Indian government gave refugees reserve stocks of horse feed—one kilo of red wheat. Milk, cooking fuel, a settlement of 4,000 rupees.

On their second day in camp, the vial of collected dirt was crushed

12

by an epileptic girl thrashing in seizure. The refugee dirt of Sindh mixed with the dirt of Kalyan and the blood of a girl. The glass glittered in the dirt and her flesh as my grandfather turned her over and extracted it from her back with long thin tweezers flashing in the blunt sunlight. The blunt sunlight. Shining on India, Pakistan, Sindh.

At night, they populated dreams of home with faces from the train, where people spoke Sindhi, ate Sindhi food, sang Sindhi songs with Sindhi mouths set in Sindhi faces. They woke to the crying of children. Coastal clouds, dark and lumpy in a sky as yellow as smoker's teeth. Their desert lungs rejected the air: too wet, too full. They took small breaths. They whispered. They told the story, over and over again, with the urgent need of new love.

—ɷ—

A year later, the family left Kalyan. My grandfather was hired as a railroad physician, a government job that came with free housing next to the tracks of his assigned station.

He treated amputations and sudden births, conductor flus, porter back-aches, malaria, tuberculosis, minor surgeries, the vice president's gout, third-class to first-class motion sickness. Among children, he was known for his compassionate hands. He folded newspapers into flying birds and put on shadow performances: his right hand, a tree; his left, a dog lifting its leg. He spoke Sindhi, Hindi, Pashto, Marathi, English, Punjabi, and ran a free clinic out of the rear of the house.

My father was the youngest child in the extended family. His sister, ten years older, his brother, seven. He often played alone at a pole in the middle of the house. The pole, riddled with pea-sized holes, was home to hundreds of ants. One of my father's enter-tainments was to set out pieces of *misri*—rock candy—and watch the ants hoist it onto their segmented backs. He skipped out the front door, past the red-faced monkeys grooming each other on the roof, and sat at the edge of the tracks mimicking lonesome steam whistles in his high-pitched voice.

Every two years, the railroad moved the family to a new house. Up and down the tracks of the countryside around Bombay they settled, uprooted, settled again. Murtazapur, Akola, Nagpur. Last of all, Thana, thirty kilometers northeast of Bombay and tucked against the Yeoor Hills.

The house in Thana, just past the railroad bridge, was surrounded by green mango trees and giant orange hibiscus bushes, the blossoms so big and heavy they bent the stalks and laid their faces on the ground. At night, the southern sky glowed with far off city lights. Fleets of fireflies rose from the grass as if answering their call. Trains in the distance, the barely detectable sound of mourning. In summer, the family dragged wooden charpoys outside and slept beneath the stars. A few cousins and uncles came to visit; sometimes they stayed a week, sometimes three years. On the west side of the house was a field and pond where Sindhi-speaking Romanis camped and washed a water buffalo. My father watched its great curved horns and sleek black hide steaming as handfuls of water flowed over its flanks. When it shook itself, its skin swung loose around its body and a spray of mist caught the sunlight. A thousand little rainbows fell through the air.

Every day, after school, my father joined my grandfather on patient visits. It was his job to carry the doctor bag and, because he was meticulous and precise, cut bandages to size and mix cough syrups. He and my grandfather were known up and down the railroad line. The doctor and his youngest son.

14

Sometimes they took the train to Mahim to see Rookie, an old friend from Sindh. A devout Hindu, Rookie spoke Sindhi with a crisp country accent. Small, plump, white-haired. Always in a sari. One morning, Rookie awakened at 5 AM to pray. She had a bath at the faucet, covered her head, sat in prayer an hour, and shuffled to the kitchen to make *mooli paratha* for breakfast. On the countertop: a basket of onions. She picked up the top onion and felt a coarse energy flow from the vegetable into her palm. The onion had changed overnight. It appeared to be growing as she held it. A large green lump sprouted from its side; thin brown skin flapped open around the white flesh. A green growth, almost a foot long, stood straight up from the top of the vegetable. She held it close to her face and cried out. It was Ganesh. Wearing a crown. Swaying over his little potbelly: a pearly white trunk lined with the dark green veins of onions. One tusk a broken stub. As she stood clutching the onion, the trunk lengthened then stopped. She fell to her knees. Placed Ganeshji in the living room niche. Garlanded him with marigolds and bells. Smeared a red *tilak* on his broad, intelligent forehead. Woke everyone to witness the miracle.

Word spread through the villages. Bombay newspapers ran the story. People arrived in droves. Thousands, every day, for weeks. Rookie did not sleep. She prayed, and ate food if it was placed in her mouth. She stayed next to Ganeshji, on the ground, at his feet. She did not let anyone touch him. After six weeks, the onion rotted, overnight, and Rookie submerged it in the sea. She became known as Onion Auntie. There was always a full basket of onions in her kitchen, though she herself never again ate one, shuddering at the thought of the knife going through its godly flesh.

—ᙢ—

January 20, 1957. My father, eleven years old, riding his bicycle around the garden in Thana. He saw my grandfather leave the compounding office and called after him, "Wait for me." My grandfather turned, said, "*Nahin, beta,* you keep playing. I will be home soon," then walked to the tracks.

15

He stood waiting on Platform Number 5, the doctor bag hanging from his right hand, the air weighted, shimmering, the strength of his wiry arms showing dark through his white shirt. He had just been to the barber. A strip of untanned skin paralleled his hairline.

That afternoon, crossing Dadar Bridge to catch the Bombay line to Churchgate, a truck ran him over and drove away. Strangers carried him, bleeding, broken, to the hospital.

There was a huge funeral along the train line, from Bombay to Kalyan Station. The light, tattered. My father too young to carry the white-shrouded body of his father to the pyre. The skin on my grandmother's face tight with grief, the whites of her eyes shocked into yellow.

During the twelve days of *puja*, throngs of people filled the house. By the pond, my father heard my great-uncle Laludada bellow to my grandmother, "Yes, of course, you must come live with us now." The railroad house, a government loan that went with the job. The family had to move from country to city; had to start over.

They took the train, free for the last time, and relocated to Merreweather Road in the heart of Bombay. A small two-bathroom, one-kitchen apartment, filled with a flux of fourteen to eighteen people.

The first few months, my father had trouble crossing the city streets. It seemed impossible, the traffic volatile. He leaned out the window at the end of the hallway and stared through the buildings at the taut sky. To be alone, he locked himself in the bathroom and looked at the walls, at the random colors of drying laundry. He fell behind in his schoolwork and suffered for his mother, widowed, in the smallest cubicle, sharing a bed with him. They lay awake at night in a desperate stillness, lost without the cacophony of trains. He thought about his father's final moments. With the glasses knocked from his face, Nanikram's last glimpse of the world: blurry, uncertain.

16

My father did all his sums for math and chemistry in chalk on his cubicle wall. He talked out loud to himself while working. Sometimes a voice floated up over the partition, *"Chha tho chain?"* What are you saying? "Nothing, just homework." He began to feel strange, a permanent visitor, living off the charity and temperamental good will of his family.

There were the usual squabbles and squeezes of a large extended household. On hard days, everyone stayed apart and Cousin Giddu played his violin, the music floating around the apartment. No one knew where he had found the violin; he was self-taught. Giddu played Deutsche Gram-mophon records for my father—Beethoven, Mozart, Bach—records he bought from an old blind man who squatted at the corner and sold music from a bamboo crate. The man ran his hands over the faces of the records, knowing each by the feel of its grooves, the spaces between songs.

My father loved Western classical music. On weekends, he borrowed Giddu's record player, placed a record on the turntable, and set the speed to 78 rpm. The slight crackle as the needle coasted over dust. He stretched out on his back, hands clasped behind his head, and drifted on the yearning, wordless tones. The music sewed his emotions together, created a moat of privacy. Clear, fractal notes hanging in the air like planets. Sometimes he sat up and focused on the bright yellow labels at the center of the records turning round and round. He missed the freedom of the countryside. The tick-tick of wheels against track shaping his days. He missed his father.

The apartment on Merreweather Road was partially owned by Uncle Laludada, a Sindhi from Quetta, near the border of Afghanistan. He was tall, bearded, loud, and had married my grandfather's eldest sister. Sometimes Laludada, equal parts charisma and bad temper, pushed his way into my father's compartment and talked over the music, his voice climbing to compete with brass and violin. He often carried a bottle of homemade sugarcane alcohol and gave sips to my father, complaining about bills and responsibilities until the record ended.

Laludada lied as easily as a hungry cat and loved like an open green bottle. A few times a day, someone's baby started screaming, and he pounded his fists on the dividing wall, his voice booming, "Why the hell don't they take care of their children?" He had owned a one-car dealership—a room so small the doors of the lone dusty Austin would not open. When the business collapsed, he stayed home and harassed the family, thriving on the chaos.

One day, Laludada stood in the doorway of his room and screamed that he wanted everyone out: "It's my house, my fucking house, all of you get out!" He grabbed my father, who was walking down the hallway, and whispered to him that the house was partly his, too. Laludada and my grandfather had bought the apartment as an investment seven years before and told the rest of their struggling brothers and sisters to move in.

My father had felt he was living on family charity. Poor fatherless Ashok, taken in out of kindness. Now he thought to himself, "I am not a guest." Laludada stood in the hallway, made a cave of his hands, and lit a cigarette. He looked at my father and said, "None of you Vaswanis will ever amount to anything."

My father went still. Vaswani was his father's name. His brother's name. His mother's and sister's name. He had always thought of Laludada as a Vaswani, too, yet here he was denouncing the family.

He stopped talking to Laludada. He was only thirteen years old, but he went silent. Listening to his mother breathe next to him in bed, the cars honking outside, my father decided he would one day leave Merreweather Road. He had never known anyone who lived alone, without family or friends. The sentence pricked against his skin, his eyelids: "None of you Vaswanis will ever amount to anything." He now had something to work for. He would become a doctor, like his father.

Over the next five years, the family fractured. Older cousins married and moved to Calcutta or Bandra, aunts died, and Laludada sold Merreweather Road. My father demanded his family's share of the sale, and my grandmother used the money to pay for his medical schooling.

—◊◊◊—

In 1964, at the age of nineteen, my father went to the housing office at Topiwala National Medical College and said, "Even though I'm from Bombay, I'm a nonresident because my family has moved and I have no place to live." The clerk rifled through a folder. The tip of his pen impressed a paper. He said, "There is a room for you in foreign housing but you will not want it." My father said, "Why not?" "Your roommate's from South Africa. His name is Deva."

"So? Give me the key." "He's an untouchable." "So? Give me the key." The clerk held the key in his hand but would not open his fist. "You'll have to spend the whole semester with him." My father pried the man's hand open and took the key. He and Deva lived together two years and played Scrabble almost every night.

My father was the first person in his class of 110 medical students to touch the dead human laid out for dissection. Five corpses floated in five tanks of formaldehyde as big as cars. A group of twenty-eight students was assigned to each body. A paper banner, limp with humidity, stretched across the front of the classroom: THE DEAD TEACH THE LIVING. Along the back wall: CHILDREN'S BONES GROW FASTER IN THE SPRINGTIME.

On the first day of class, the teacher swung his pointer over a *mungi*, a black biting ant, crawling on his desk. He told the class of Shushruta, a sixth-century BC doctor who used *mungi* during intestinal surgery. Pinching them, alive and wriggling, he touched the ants to an open incision. When the ants bit down, Shushruta clipped their bodies from their locked jaws. Absorbable, natural sutures. "The lesson is: use everything," the teacher said, and turned a crank on each tank, raising the cadavers from the formaldehyde then lowering them onto galvanized steel tables shining in the fluorescent light. He said, "Start cutting," and left the room.

The formaldehyde planed off the tables and ran in fast streams along the floor to the drain at the center of the classroom. The students held hankies to their faces against the stench of pickled death. Most of them were upper caste and wealthy and adhered to the caste system in their daily lives. But, to get through medical school, they had to touch a corpse. Every day, four hours, for six months.

My father sat for a minute, then abruptly stood and laid his hands on the dead man closest to him. His father's trade, passed on. He believed in the vocation of medicine. Science and compassion. The art of the human form. If, to know that better, he had to touch the dead, so be it. He set to work by himself. One by one, the rest of the students joined him.

They named their body Pawan because of his fast-looking runner's legs. Six students worked on Pawan's arms, six on his legs, six on his abdomen, six on his chest, four on his head. The abdomen team worked with the arm team so they wouldn't get in each other's way. Chest and leg came in together. The head team arrived whenever, and shared with the dental school. Everyone rotated to a different quadrant of the body throughout the semester. By the end of six months, each person had dissected an entire cadaver.

Once the work started, the students grew used to it and cracked jokes. They salivated at deltoids like salmon. Biceps pink and lean as chicken cutlets. Intricate embroidered nerves. The beige and spongy heart: an involuntary muscle, its own willful thing. They laughed at the bladder, the size of a plum, "No wonder we are always having to pee."

They unpacked the body. The tongue and its sixteen muscles. The butterfly-shaped sphenoid bone connecting to every bone in the skull except the mandible. Pawan's was large; his voice must have been resonant as a cave. He had been a smoker, his larynx covered in little bumps like a toasted marshmallow. Shoulders flanging wide and sturdy. A rash from a rengas tree on his hands. The straight uncomplicated route of his digestive tract, from mouth to anus. When they opened his skull and saw his brain, they said the word in unison: *stroke*. There, a dark spread through the tissue. They stood over him, silent. His muscles laid out on the table like wings.

The cadaver next to theirs was a woman. She was lithe and tall, a long poem. You could see she had been graceful by the way her knees cocked. Her pelvis was somehow erotic. She seemed more human, less specimen, than the others, as if a bit of her soul still lurked beneath her skin. She had died twenty-four weeks pregnant. The baby tucked inside her, a girl, a perfect fit to the womb. When they shined a flashlight behind the baby's hand, her bones glowed red. Tiny as the legs of spiders.

They named the baby Kalpana. *Imagination.* At the end of each day, someone different drew the shades, sang her a lullaby, and then turned off the lights and locked the door of the lab.

—⚏—

In 1965, tensions over the still undefined states of Jammu and Kashmir erupted. What became known as the Second Kashmir War, or the Indo-Pak War of 1965, was not, militaristically speaking, large-scale, although approximately 6,800 lives were lost in a series of skirmishes and bungled operations.

While historians tend to agree that Bombay was never besieged, my father recalls an oppressive time of suspicion and bunker mentality. Topiwala National Medical College, against the Arabian Sea and flanked by fields, was considered a choice area for mines, bombs, submarine landings, and parachuting Pakistanis. My father and most of the other male students joined the army, and all medical students, women included, were asked to aid in the war effort. They went out into Bombay neighborhoods and painted the top half of civilian headlights black, to reduce light. They raided the hospital storehouse, bursting with boxes of defunct medical files, and took scissors to old X-rays. They snipped around the clear white of bone and healthy tissue, using only the spaces between ribs, black of tumors, opaque livers. They collaged the dark and grey pieces together on windows, blocking indoor light from streets.

After class, in the evenings, my father donned his khaki uniform and patrolled a five-mile area with a *lathi*, beating rhythms into his palm as he walked. The moon rose blurred and blood red. He marched the coastline, football fields, racecourse, cricket fields, peering into the darkness, sweeping the ground for mines, watching the sky for planes, the black shushing sea for boats. When he heard gunfire, he lay on his face in the dirt. He had nothing but the baton to fight with. Once he heard something following him. His flashlight illuminated a fox—ribs stark through patchy fur, clouded cataract eyes. It looked at him and sat down like a dog, starving. My father squatted and shined his flashlight into a thick stand of grass. Watched the fox pounce, hunting for mice, moles, or nothing, in the long white beam. By three in the morning, he returned to his dorm and sat in the room with Deva behind the random bits of quilted X-rays. They discussed Dr. Hiranandani, who performed seven-minute tonsillectomies with no blood. His fascinating use of adverbs, such as *this adenoid is prototypically small.*

Wherever Sindh was, wherever it had been, my father was defending India. But he was always careful to avoid anti-Pakistan and anti-Muslim sentiment. He was a traditional Sindhi, part Muslim, part Sikh, part Hindu, part Buddhist, and had been educated by Jesuits. Religion was fluid in his family and community—Sindh, an ancient cultural melting pot and the cradle of the Indus-Valley civilization. My father understood that it was the mistakes of governments and individual hatred that caused Partition. As much as his refugee heart ached to return home, he never allowed himself to lay blame. He believed in the pluralism of India.

Ultimately, the five-month Indo-Pak War was considered a draw. India gained 1,184 km (710 miles) of Pakistani territory, and Pakistan gained 545 km (210 miles) of Indian territory, and both sides inflated the numbers. Rumor and innuendo replaced reality. The Indian warship that Pakistan claimed to have trapped in Bombay Harbor was in fact in dry dock for repairs. An Indian general's claims to have used almost all the ammunition at the front lines turned out to be wrong to the tune of eighty-five percent.

In his last year of medical school, my father did a rural rotation, performing mass injections of streptomycin and aspirin on tuberculosis patients in villages across Maharashtra. The streptomycin soaked in through his fingers in large quantities; he developed lifelong tinnitus. His fellow students called him "the American" because of his good English, affinity for Pat Boone, and democratic egalitarianism. When he grew out his hair like John Lennon, they called him *hajaam*, barber, with a fond irony. He was slender as a broom, constant ringing in both ears. He loved constellations that wheeled into predictable spots in the sky and the unexpectedness of a shooting star. Diseases that manifested as published and tumor anomalies. The planned and unplanned, both.

Twenty-five years old, he graduated with a medical degree. That night, celebrating over a beer with a cousin, he learned his father had been murdered. It was often done that way: hire a truck to mow someone down. Everyone in the family knew, everyone but my father, who had been a boy at the time of his father's death. The family believed the murderer was a distant relative, someone who owed my grandfather money. His book of accounts, the small sums he had loaned friends and family, without interest, had disappeared the same day he died and never been found.

The news broke my father. A feral sorrow crawled into his chest. His gentle, beloved father, murdered, and the truth kept from him. His sense of trust, shaken. Another home destroyed.

It was 1970 and my father was a young doctor seeking a job in a parched Indian economy—20,000 unemployed physicians and a surplus of 100,000 engineers. Like so many of his generation, he was enamored with the idea of America; he decided to take the ECFMG exams (Educational Council for Foreign Medical Graduates), which the U.S. government required of immigrant doctors. The two exam sites closest to India were Afghanistan and Sierra Leone. If he made it to Freetown, Sierra Leone, he could stay with his cousin Pratap who worked at Chainrai and Company, a small Sindhi-run supermarket in the city center. There he could take the exam, and, if he passed, go on to America.

My father wanted to go to the United States because it was not England. He intended to learn Western medical practices and return home when job opportunities improved. He bought a ticket to Sierra Leone. His first plane ride. His mother, brother, sister came from Calcutta to see him off at the airport. They held each other, in a circle, for a long time. He took with him an American medical textbook, as heavy as a newborn baby, and one small suitcase, the size of a pillow. Black plastic handle, black plastic sides, red and black plaid face bordered by black zipper. Bombay Tartan. Cheap, functional, hybrid. Red as the *sindhoor* in a married woman's hair.

He arrived in Freetown on June 20, and moved in with his cousin. The Sindhi way. A network of uprooted family. When he wasn't studying for the exam, he played cricket behind the university with a gang of doctors running in flapping white coats and stethoscopes, the sky twisting from metallic grey to burning pink as they bowled and batted around a herd of grazing goats with a penchant for chewing on wickets. Once a week the doctors lugged an old projector to the Lebanese ex-pat pub and ran movies against the back stucco wall that pimpled the faces of

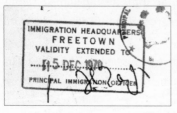

movie stars. Everyone's favorite was a pirated television reel—ten episodes of an American show called *Star Trek*. My father loved Spock, his pointy ears and rationality. He and the Freetowners catcalled so loud for Lieutenant Uhura, no one knew what her voice sounded like.

My father was playing snooker at the pub when the cholera epidemic broke out. The first known case diagnosed on a cargo ship in the Port of Call. He heard about it from the bartender, dialed the international operator, and asked for the Center for Disease Control in Atlanta. He said to the woman on the other end of the line, "Hello, my name is Dr. Vaswani. I am phoning from Sierra Leone where a cholera epidemic has just reached." The CDC took his cousin's address and promised to mail vaccines. Two days later, 1,500 vaccines in a military crate stamped with the American flag arrived at the basement door of Mr. Chainrai's house. The dry ice steamed as my father lifted the Styrofoam lid. The cold and burning scent of particles realigned.

He and a doctor friend borrowed a car and packed the heat-sensitive vaccines into the backseat, shading the windows with black burkas borrowed from a Muslim neighbor. They immunized the docks and the entire western half of Freetown. After the second day of immunizing, when they entered a neighborhood, people stood waiting for them in a zigzag line, sleeves pushed up, arms extended. The final number of cholera cases in Sierra Leone in 1970 was reported at 340, with forty-seven deaths. In neighboring Ghana, there were 16,000 cases and 829 deaths.

The next week, my father passed the exam and applied for a U.S. work visa. He had been away from India and his immediate family for seven months, and was now accustomed to being alone, to washing his underwear and socks in the sink every night.

The day he left Freetown was the day Sierra Leone switched from driving on the left side of the road to the right, to celebrate ten years of freedom from the British. The streets bristled with raucous energy. Mass chaos and collision. Signs were dragged down, moved to the opposite side of the street, mixed-up and re-bolted to the wrong pole. An entire city lost, confused, delighted, free. It took my father six hours to go thirty miles to the airport. When he speaks of it now, pride rings his voice. He always says the same thing: "It was a mess. But it was *their* mess."

He was on his way to the United States.

—⁂—

America's first documented Indian immigrant jumped off a merchant clipper in 1790, freestyled ashore at Salem, Massachusetts, and is described in history books as *an unnamed man from Madras who disappeared into the slave population*. Between 1820 and 1898, 523 more Indians immigrated to North America, most converted Christian slaves or indentured servants from colonial England. Between 1898 and 1913, Punjabi famine and American labor needs conspired to bring 7,000 Indian farmers to the United States. In 1907, under the auspices of the Asian Exclusion League, several hundred Americans destroyed Indian living quarters in Bellingham and Everett, Washington, and then attacked and drove the immigrants from the cities— acts sanctioned by local police and President Theodore Roosevelt. Ten years later, Congress passed a law citing all of Asia a barred immigration zone, and in 1923 the Supreme Court legislated Indian policy with *United States v. Bhagat Singh Thind*, a case that categorized Indians as "not white people," meaning a population Congress had never intended for naturalization. This ruling had a fourfold effect: Indians were denied citizenship, previous naturalizations were annulled and deemed illegal, Indian landowners in California (where the bulk of the population lived) were forbidden from buying or leasing land, and previous land purchases were revoked. By 1940, the number of Indians in America had dropped to 2,405. Many married into the Mexican-American community.

Truman's pen outranked the Thind decision with the Luce–Cellar Act of July 3, 1946. An annual Indian immigration quota was set at 100 per year. This legislation remained status quo until October of 1965, when, standing at the base of the Statue of Liberty, flanked by two Kennedys hunched against the blowsy Harbor wind, Lyndon Baines Johnson signed the Immigration and Naturalization Act.

The 1965 Immigration Act was my father's point of entry into the United States. The Act offered quotas for families and educated professionals to enter the country and work. At the time, the United States suffered a shortage of native doctors and engineers, and turned to immigration to solve its labor crisis.

—∞—

January 29, 1971. On the plane to New York, my father wore all his socks at once, three pair, causing his Bata sandals to squeeze in the toes. He arrived to snow-frosted pavement. The air crackled with the harsh scent of jet fuel.

He felt a slight vertigo as he looked out the window of the cab, taking in the orderly pace of traffic, the great distance between buildings. The taxi drove him twenty-five miles northeast into Long Island, dropping him off at the Glen Cove Hospital Emergency Room. He stood in front of the doors, on the sidewalk, gripping his suitcase. The doors slid apart, suddenly. Like *Star Trek*. Futuristic. No need to stop and fumble when wheeling a gurney. A secretary ran forward, "Oh! You're here! From India!" She handed him a key that seemed too small and sleek to be real.

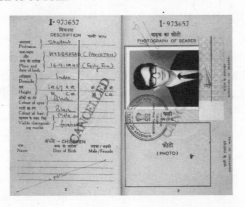

At intern housing, my father lay down on a naked mattress and shivered himself to sleep. When he woke up, he walked. On the streets, no honking, no muezzins, no goats. Just a few cars rolling by on silent, thick tires. One crow, perched on a light post. *Kawaa*, he said to it. The smell of wet wool in a grey landscape under a sky that looked sketched. He walked six miles, and saw a brick building with a white cupola: FRIENDLY'S. The heavy door sucked against his pull, his feet sank into thick carpeting. Salt and pepper shakers on every table. Long luxurious paper napkins. The waitresses gathered by the coffee machine to look at him. A different one wandered over every few minutes and asked if he was ready to order. Finally, a little blonde approached. He liked the coconut waft of her shampoo, how her skirt lay over her pantyhose. He calculated the time it would take his body to metabolize a Fribble and decided, yes, it was the cheapest and most sensible thing to eat.

At Glen Cove Hospital, where he would later meet my mother in a waiting room, my father worked six-and-a-half days a week, double shifts, and blinked in bright sunlight. He was known among interns as an intuitive diagnoser, reading a patient's breath, pupils, gait. He considered his patients sick people, not Americans. The body is always the same in its need, function, and response to disease. The body never lies.

He converted everything into litres, kilos, Celsius, in order to understand its true quantity. For a while, he slept on a piece of wax paper ripped from an examining room table, then borrowed a set of sheets from the ICU. He met a nurse with a long, horsey face and grey eyes that slanted. She wore gardenia perfume, like his sister. He watched for the elevator doors to close behind her before pressing the up arrow. When the elevator returned to his floor, he stepped into the small space and inhaled the concentrated scent of his sister.

In March, at the end of a two-day shift, he walked out through the automatic doors of the ER. On the other side, under a lukewarm sun, he realized he had not felt his customary nervous flutter. The doors had glided apart and he had walked through, unthinking. For the next few weeks, he had a recurring dream of standing in a long line, waiting for something, a family of women behind him speaking a dialect known only to themselves. Once he dreamt in kilograms, a whole dream where he spoke nothing but kilograms and the trees whispered in his father's voice.

On the way to the ICU, on the second floor of Glen Cove Hospital, there was a waiting room. Green plastic chairs, muted green walls, two fake ficus trees. Near the end of a shift, an hour before midnight, on March 31st, 1971, my father passed that room. In the second chair from the wall, long dark hair falling toward her book, sat a young woman.

—⚏—

28

My mother was born in Manhattan in 1948, but from the age of five, she was a child of the largest island in the contiguous United States.

Long Island: 118 miles long and twenty-three miles wide, stretching just east of Manhattan and northeast into the Atlantic Ocean. Its history is one of influx and changing demographics: from Lenape, Shinnecock, Corchaug, and Montauk, to Dutch, British, and American. Until the 1883 completion of the Brooklyn Bridge, the only connection between Long Island and the rest of the country was by boat. The island remained largely rural, covered in pine forests and small farms, until an advertisement ran in *Newsday* on May 7th, 1947, offering 2,000 homes for sixty dollars a month in a new development on open plains. By the end of May, more than 6,500 veterans had filed applications for the housing units of Levittown—the first town in the United States to mass-produce houses for GIs returning home from war.

Nassau County, Long Island, changed from agrarian pastures to the nation's largest suburb. From 1950 to 1960, the population doubled to 1,300,700. The majority of the new inhabitants were Italian and Irish Catholic, and Jewish American. Postwar Long Island culture was marked by the unique cohabitation and mixing of these groups.

The town where my mother grew up, Hicksville, Long Island, was named for Valentine Hicks, a member of a famous abolitionist and Quaker family and the second president of the Long Island Railroad. Hicksville began as a station stop in 1837, and was a long-standing depot for produce, particularly pickles. After a blight destroyed the pickle crop on Long Island, farmers in the area switched to potatoes, a crop that continued to thrive throughout my mother's childhood. Contemporary Hicksville is home to Nassau County's Little India, but during my mother's time, it was a Catholic enclave in an old Protestant stronghold.

—m—

My Irish family's American history begins and ends in New York. My grandfather grew up at the far end of Flatbush Avenue, Brooklyn, back when it had more cows than people. My grandmother's family, the Sullivans, came from Ireland in 1897 and settled in a tenement apartment in the neighborhood of Hell's Kitchen, Manhattan. There were eleven Sullivan children (nine living): Jo, Kay, Bea, Peggy, Julia, Mary, Jimmy, Dan, Bart. The girls shared one bed, sleeping like stacked spoons, and the boys shared another. They grew up on two meals of bread and butter a day, a steady stream of Communion wafers, and, at Christmas, one extravagant orange each. The youngest girl, Julia, my grandmother, finished high school and was the only child who didn't turn over her wages to help feed the family.

My great-grandfather, James Sullivan, made his living breaking rock for the Manhattan Bridge. My great-grandmother, Catherine Sullivan, was a washerwoman, an unwavering, Irish matriarch. When her first child Bart was two, there was no one to take care of him. But she was pregnant again and needed money, so she tied the boy up in the chicken coop behind the tenement and went off to work. "It was fine," my mother always said when telling this story. "He was safe there. There was nothing else to be done. Besides, for the rest of his life he loved chickens."

It was an economic coup when my grandfather, Elwood, and my grandmother, Julia, moved to Long Island in 1953 and put their two children in Catholic schools. By then, my uncle Woody was eleven, and my mother, five. A Catholic education, the cleansing and firm influence of nuns, had been an unaffordable dream of my great-grandparents.

Julia's suburban relocation capped the Sullivan rise from poverty. All her sisters and brothers came to take stock of the Hicksville house. My mother remembers her Uncle Jimmy arriving in his WWII uniform; he always thumbed a ride faster in navy togs. He stood in the Hicksville bathroom and looked around: pink laminate counter speckled with gold, pink muslin curtain hanging at the window, framing a pink dogwood planted just outside. Pink toilet paper. Jimmy put his big square hands on the counter, laughed, and said, "We're moving up in the world. Wiping our arses with pink tissue paper instead of the headlines."

My mother recreated that pink bathroom in every apartment and house we lived in—more than thirteen homes in eighteen years. A coat of pink paint, a pair of pink towels, pink soap in a pink soap dish. A roll of pink toilet paper perched on the back of the toilet, and a cheaper white roll on the spindle. Whenever we had company, expected or unexpected, the white roll miraculously disappeared and was replaced with the pink. When company left, the white roll returned. I knew my mother was comfortable with someone if she left the white roll on the spindle. She dropped appearances. Showed her thriftiness, upbringing. She never forgot the Sullivan lesson that toilet paper is a luxury.

—◊—

My grandfather was an accountant, but, on a whim, in 1953, he put all his money into a rifle-parts factory on Long Island. He ran it for five profitable years before it burned to the ground in a suspicious fire that left him in debt and unemployed. The police believed the fire was arson because my grandfather had just been elected to the Hicksville Board of Education—their first ever Irish-Catholic. He had run for office to get free bussing for Catholic children, like his son and daughter, who were minorities in a community with a large Ku Klux Klan membership.

A week after the fire, my grandmother went to the dentist to get an abscessed tooth pulled and was told she had stage-three mouth cancer.

It was 1957 and my mother was nine years old.

31

My grandfather said God had forsaken them and yanked the Sacred Heart of Jesus off the living room wall before leaving for church. When he returned, the Sacred Heart of Jesus was back on the wall and the Sullivan sisters and brothers filled the living room sofa and chairs. They drank coffee and swapped miracles:

> Mrs. Garrity from the old neighborhood who took in sewing till she saved enough for a coach seat to Spain. She stood before St. Teresa of Avila's thumb, a crooked arthritic bone sealed in wax, and her emphysema disappeared in a blue zag of light.

> Great-uncle Timmy, as Irish as Paddy's Pig, who lost his teeth on the subway tracks and ate nothing but soup for six years and prayed to St. Jude every night. One morning he awoke with sparkling gums, pink as taffy, and teeth like a wealthy child. Praise be.

And so on.

My grandfather knelt on the living room floor, Julia's ringed hand dangling over the side of her chair and moving like a moody river through his hair. He crooned her name as only he could: Jool-ya, Jool-ya.

He sold the scorched factory land and got a job working for Federal Home Loan auditing books for banks. He stayed on the road five days a week, traveling from bank to bank throughout the South, living out of his Buick to save money for hospital bills and the children's Catholic educations. His diabetes worsened. He shrugged before eating a doughnut as if weighing the consequences, then accepting them. He lost a kidney. Had a heart attack. Recovered from colon cancer. He ironed his shirtsleeves against the backs of doors in gas station bathrooms and, on weekends,

drove seven hundred miles north to take my grandmother to radiation treatments. He dressed in pink and white suits and glossy shoes, a white fedora with a yellow band. My grandmother said only a man as broad and red-haired as Elwood S. Kent could get away with that.

—⁂—

Julia was known for her electric wit, straight-talk, and lustrous beauty. Like the rest of the Sullivans, she had jet-black hair, dark brown eyes, and a milky complexion—Black Irish looks. She started smoking in 1924 to show she was as good as a man. She was tall for a woman, 5'9", with long legs she accentuated with pumps made for walking to work in Union Square or dancing at Harlem clubs. Her dazzling smiles were the pride of the family. White and even, what Jimmy called "star teeth."

My mother said men would often halt in the street to stare at my grandmother. She was beautiful like birdsong that people fall silent to hear. Unknown women on the subway spilled their secrets to her, random children and dogs pressed against her legs. She was magnetic, a blend of tough and tender. The Sullivans were generous and affectionate, but they were also a brawly bunch, holding grudges for decades, throwing unexpected punches, acting out petty jealousies. When the family came to Hicksville, especially the uncles, Julia leaned in the doorway and said, "When you're in my house, you don't fight." And they didn't. Everyone called her The

Peacemaker. A veil of calm descended in her presence. She was a woman of her word; if they fought in her house, she would not hesitate to throw them out. They sent their sons and daughters to her for wry, profound advice. And the sicker she got, the more the family valued her opinion. She never complained or asked for anything. Her only sign of bitterness was toward her religion; she stopped going to church but insisted that my mother and uncle continue, saying: "Do as I say, not as I do."

—⁓—

In the 1950s, the five-year survival rate for women with stage-three mouth cancer was nine percent. My grandmother lived thirteen years. Chemotherapy was not used at the time, and radiation was new and barbaric. Treatments took pieces of patients, bone by bone.

My grandmother's oncologist would sit across from her, smoking, and tell her not to smoke. He recommended she switch to filtered cigarettes and try different brands till she found one less addictive. On her doctor's advice, she tried Chesterfields, Kools, Parliaments, Camels, Winstons, Virginia Slims, and Pall Malls.

The first assault on Julia's body was two days after her diagnosis. Radiation treatments cause teeth to rot and create a risk of infection, so the oral cancer protocol, pre-radiation, is removal. Every single one of my grandmother's teeth, all of them healthy, were pulled—her bottom teeth one day, her top the next. Her jaw bone was filed smooth and her face mummified in padding and gauze.

She lost forty pounds, and quit her job as a bookkeeper for the florist division of the Brooklyn Diocese, but still dressed every morning for work. She sat on the couch, in a baggy pencil skirt and blouse, a pen tucked behind her ear, a smoking Parliament like a sixth finger on her bony right hand, and her purse beside her. She kept her cigarettes in her purse because she always had and because, one day, she might get better.

My grandfather turned Julia's radiation treatments into big city excursions. He would arrive home late Friday night, usually from South

Carolina or Georgia. On Saturday morning, he rousted my mother, uncle, and grandmother into the Buick and drove them over the Kosciuszko Bridge to Brooklyn and Long Island College Hospital. A nurse took my grandparents behind a lead door marked: DANGER: RADIATION. Another nurse brought a chair for my uncle Woody to stand on, then picked up my mother so she could see through the tiny glass window. The children looked through as Julia was strapped down under a betatron radiation machine. The nurse said, "See now, everything will be okay. The doctors are helping your mommy." They watched as my grandmother's head was tightened into an iron mask and a long thin tube that looked like a gun was pointed at her jaw.

After the radiation treatments, my grandfather took the family to Gage and Tollner's, a famous steak restaurant on Fulton Street in Brooklyn that maintained its original nineteenth-century décor. A long room with mirrored walls and mahogany tables, menus like bound books, live piano music, and handsome men in white jackets who parked the Buick and brought my mother Shirley Temples bobbing with shiny red cherries. In winter, there was turtle soup and gas lighting. The family could not afford the restaurant but lunches were cheaper than dinners and it was something to look forward to, something separate from the horror of radiation. My grandmother chewed her meat carefully. Her dentures didn't fit her filed jaw; she said they felt like a mouthful of rocks. She never ate much after her teeth were removed, and usually gave my mother and uncle half of everything on her plate. She liked to crack jokes about McCarthy coming after her. They all associated radiation with infiltration, dead Japanese, bomb shelters, and the Cincinnati Reds changing their name so as not to appear unpatriotic.

The day after a radiation treatment, the burn scars on Julia's neck, jaw, and shoulders turned purplish and she would be overwhelmed with nausea and vomiting. She said radiation tasted and smelled like a combination of a rusty metal rake and burnt flesh. She developed food allergies and became too weak to cook, although she would, by sheer force of will, make dinner every Friday night. She hated fish and had

35

grown sensitive to the smell of it, so she declared Catholic Fridays "World Cuisine Night," and whipped up recipes from her old Hell's Kitchen neighbors: Italians, Swedes, Ukrainians, Armenians, Germans. My mother and uncle would research each country at the library and read out snippets of history between bites.

In 1957, the year my grandmother was diagnosed, the Surgeon General stated that evidence pointed to a mild relationship between smoking and lung cancer. A Gallup Survey conducted in 1958 found that only forty-four percent of Americans believed smoking caused cancer. In 1969, the year after my grandmother died, cigarette advertising on television and radio was banned, and in 1970 the warning label on cigarette packs was made in the name of the United States Surgeon General.

—⚏—

After a few months of radiation, my grandmother had surgery that removed half of her jawbone, half of her tongue, and the lymph nodes in her neck. She came home with her entire head bandaged except for her eyes. It looked like someone had taken lopsided bites out of her. Her cheeks, collapsed.

She was mortified by the devastation of her beauty. She called her doctors "monster-makers" and avoided mirrors. The few times she left the house, people stared in shock and fear. My mother would hold my grandmother's hand and fiercely stare down strangers. She was ten years old in 1958—the year *Reader's Digest* published an article saying cancer was contagious. The children at school shunned her and their parents wouldn't let her come to their houses. Only the nuns weren't afraid.

It was difficult for my grandmother to talk with an incomplete tongue and jaw. Her words sat in the air like the stumps of trees. As her voice receded, her face grew more expressive. Scowls, smiles burst across her sunken cheeks like summer storms. Her index finger: a bloodcurdling scream. She spoke in shotgun blasts. *Bed Now. Love You. Stop That. Good.* She sat on the couch, and the family swirled around her. A cigarette, long ashed, in her right hand. One elbow buried deep in a pillow. Every crisis, tragedy, venial sin, went past her.

My mother understood my grandmother's language and translated for doctors, nurses, priests, family, as if Julia were foreign. When the uncles and aunts crossed the bridges and tunnels for a Saturday Sullivan party, Julia could no longer stand to greet them, but she picked the records and danced the Charleston seated, legs kicking sideways, head thrown back, singling out the trumpet and following its voice with her hips.

At age eleven, my mother took on the responsibilities of cooking and cleaning. She watched everything from atop a wooden stool at the kitchen sink. Chapped hands in scalding water, piles of flowered dishes and copper-bottomed pots. When the dishes shone and dripped on the dry-rack, she scrubbed the sink and starched her brother's and father's shirts. She liked them to stand up like soldiers. Like nuns in their wimples.

She turned the living room couch to face the kitchen and my grandmother propped herself up and taught my mother how to make Sunday dinner: a capon, creamed pearl onions, and cauliflower with cheese sauce. When Julia didn't have the energy to talk, she wrote out recipes, and said, her voice going in and out like a fuzzy radio station: "If you can read, you can cook."

My uncle Woody cheered them both. He had joined the track team but there was no afterschool bussing and my grandmother could not drive to pick him up. So on track nights, he would hitchhike home from Mineola, picking up rides on Jericho Turnpike and the Northern State, usually arriving in time for dinner. He'd come in with funny stories about the people who had driven him home. A half dozen men with wedding rings put their hands on his leg or said something suggestive. At least a dozen Jehovah Witnesses and/or Mormons tried to convert him. Once a woman tried to sell him a pet cheetah that was stretched out in the backseat of her Chevy. He would come home and act out the situations, leaving Julia and my mother breathless with laughter.

Woody was brilliant but reclusive. When he was ten years old, he read the entire children's section of the Hicksville Library. He won a free trip to the U.N. for doing so and was the first child in Hicksville to be given an adult library card (with the condition he not read anything dirty). He let my mother count his freckles, and introduced her to Willa Cather, his favorite author. But he would often withdraw and didn't have many friends. His ears stuck out and when the kids at Sunday School called him Dumbo, my mother fought them with her fists and teeth. The nuns said, "She's a Sullivan, all right," and sent her to confession. Even though

she was a Kent, Sheila Kent, she—and her father and brother—were always Sullivans, as if her mother's blood and presence eclipsed all else.

Sometimes she found her brother in the kitchen, staring into the flame of a candle. He did that for hours, without moving or speaking. Once he threw a butcher knife at her. Once they sat on the front steps listening to birds. He told her what human ears hear as music is nothing but avian war-mongering. His bouts of shyness and suspicion intensified but so did his brilliance. People always noticed his intelligence but no one except his eighth grade teacher, Sister Mary Kevin, who called one night during the dinner hour, ever suggested mental illness.

It wasn't until after Vietnam, after he moved to Arkansas, married, and had a child, that he had his first schizophrenic break.

—∞—

My mother's closest friend was her cousin John, who was three years her junior and lived down the street. He walked over to the house almost every afternoon and sat at the kitchen table with his owl glasses, crisp shirt, acerbic wit, and copy of Modern Teen with Bobby Rydell on the cover that he smooched when he thought no one was looking. My grandmother let him smoke her cigarettes and talk like Montgomery Clift playing Father William Logan in *I Confess*. He ran away from school a few times a week and sat at the kitchen table with Julia, pouring out his heart, waving his hands like language, like opera. When Julia talked on the telephone, he liked to dance the Limbo under the cord stretched across the kitchen to try and make her laugh. Sometimes he stood quietly and watched the phone cord dip into a pot of goulash boiling on the stove, the bubbles breaking in soft pops, like souls released.

If there were bruises on John's arms, Julia called his father and berated him and John spent a few nights sleeping on a cot in my mother's room. Those nights, the family stayed up late and ran old home movies against the kitchen wall, watching the Sullivans in their twenties, tap-dancing on the roof in Hell's Kitchen to aggravate the Italian neighbors downstairs. There was the old patriarch, James Sullivan; his hard wife, Catherine; the eight older siblings; and Julia, the baby girl of the family, dark eyes flashing, black hair blowing, the buildings of the city and grainy sky rising behind her.

In the dim kitchen, Julia's cigarette smoke wafted in the triangle of projector light. It was not my grandmother's flickering beauty that made my mother and John cry. It was that she moved without wincing, without pain. It was the realization that there is always a Before and an After.

—※—

My grandmother was a reader, a self-educator. Every Sunday after church she sent my mother to the library with a list of seven books, one for each day of the week. She said the library was church without the collection plate. She sat on the couch and read, using just her eyes and fingers, which still had life in them.

The Hicksville Library was two-and-a-half miles away from the house. My mother would walk there, stopping to pick up John. They'd swing their arms in unison and talk about everything. They'd rest at the public school (an exotic, forbidden place), and stand on the cavernous front steps to echo their voices. On the way back home from the library, my mother would carry three of Julia's library books, and John would carry four.

The seven library books sat stacked on top of the piano that no one in the family could play. When Julia finished a book, she put it at the bottom of the pile. When pain gripped her, she closed her eyes and threw things. A small red mark above the TV from *East of Eden*. A black smudge near the front door from *Exodus*.

On radiation weeks, Julia only left the couch to retch in the pink bathroom. She tented her book on the coffee table, lurched to the toilet. When she returned, she picked up the book and read the same sentence over and over, her eyes moving in slow ticks like a typewriter then pushing back to the front of the line. My mother rubbed dollops of Jergens into the radiation burns on Julia's shoulders, careful not to wobble the book in her hands.

It was on Jack Paar that Julia first heard of *Lady Chatterley's Lover* and *Mrs. 'Arris Goes to Paris*. Both in violation of the Legion of Decency—a listing of books and movies that rotted your brain, infected your soul, curved your spine, and kept the country from winning the war—printed on the back page of *Long Island Catholic*, the newspaper my grandmother read cover to cover every week.

Julia read *Lady Chatterley's Lover* on a Wednesday, around three packs of Pall Malls. She propped the book on her knee and dipped her face down to it, eyes moving fast, hands light and tender against the pages.

My mother went to bed before Julia finished the book, and at breakfast, asked if she had liked it. "It's beautifully written," my grandmother said. "I can't see what all the other fuss is over. It's about living your own life. And a rich woman loving a poor man."

My mother slipped *Lady Chatterley's Lover* from the bottom of the pile and brought it to school. All day, she felt the book burning a hole in her schoolbag. She felt the nuns could smell it. It took her three nights, reading in her closet with a flashlight and a pile of batteries, her dry aching eyes flying across the sentences. An hour after she had slipped the book back to the bottom of the pile, her mother casually asked, "So, how was it?" My mother blushed and stammered. Julia said, "I thought so, too."

My mother returned the book late to the library. She did not have money with her and the librarian, a brittle woman with eyes like sunflower seeds, took pity on her and waived the fee.

When she told my grandmother, Julia slapped her and sent her back to the library with the last dollar bill from her purse and a note: *Thank you for your kind gesture. We do not take charity. We take responsibility for our actions. Please excuse this late book.*

—◊◊—

The year my mother turned thirteen, a nun paddled her open palm for asking why God allowed slavery. Her cousin John went with her to buy her first bra, her father gave her a silver charm bracelet dangling with the word HOPE, her mother lost another quarter of her jaw and tongue to surgery, her brother got a 1600 on his SAT and a full scholarship to Notre Dame (the first boy in the family to go to college), and Uncle Jimmy divorced and remarried.

Uncle Jimmy was my grandmother's favorite brother. He had a prescient streak, and believed in dreams, fairies, and gut instinct. He always set his table for ghosts: an empty chair with a pillow for back support; an extra plate, knife, fork, glass. He was the Sullivan baby boy:

41

black-headed, black-eyed, with a thrice-broken nose. He worked as a waiter at the swanky Stork Club on 53rd Street and owned a white Studebaker convertible that he drove with the top down, rain or shine. He'd won a rickety little motorboat playing the ponies and liked to take the family out on weekends, especially when the radio predicted bad weather. Bobbing on the choppy Long Island Sound, he guzzled beers in five swallows and told hateful stories of the war. It was a kind of therapy, everyone out on the creaking boat, eyeing the rearing whitecaps as Jimmy drank and talked.

One weekend, a storm came in fast. Clouds stacked the horizon, sucking the light from the sky. Waves slopped onto their feet and the rusty old motor stalled. The women shrieked at Jimmy. He got down on his knees and poured a Coke over the engine. It sizzled at the rust and the boat started up. Jimmy laughed: "You should see how much it takes to start an aircraft carrier." The women threw their shoes at him, and he turned the boat south, driving fast and bumpy over the waves till my mother thought her stomach would heave out her mouth and fly backward to Connecticut. By the time they got to shore, Uncle Jimmy was what the family called Gallic Drunk. Aunt Edna teased and hugged him while sliding the car keys from his pocket. He heard the jingle, drew his fist back to hit her. When my grandfather stepped between them, Edna reached around him and gave Jimmy the keys.

Uncle Jimmy had fallen in love with Edna at thirteen, and got her pregnant at sixteen. No one could figure out where they'd managed to do it with twelve people in a tiny Hell's Kitchen apartment. "Where there's a will, there's a way," my mother always said.

They were married at seventeen. Later, after the navy, after the war, Jimmy divorced Edna for a Swedish woman named Lillian, who looked and acted Irish with her flaming red hair and relentless jokes. When Edna found out about Lillian, she sat out on her fire escape and drank a bottle of bleach. She didn't die but for the rest of her life she spoke in a whisper—the bleach had seared the lining of her throat.

Before moving upstate, Edna came to Hicksville to see Julia. They sat on the couch and gossiped in their ravaged voices. "The pain of love and the pain of cancer," they laughed to each other in wheezes. On the coffee table, they spread an assembly line of food and made the children's Friday Catholic lunches: tuna fish, and date bread with cream cheese.

Jimmy and Edna's two children never forgave him and he didn't try too hard to mend the wounds. He and Lillian, who was childless, chose my mother as their pet. When Jimmy got free tickets from famous restaurant patrons wanting a good table, he and Lillian took my mother to plays and musicals. Whenever she went out with them, she came home floating. It was a respite from housework and her mother's long struggle.

—◊—

In 1963, my mother was greasing the kitchen window tracks with Vaseline to combat the salty island air that swelled the wood every spring. She looked outside and saw my grandmother digging in the yard. Exhausted, skeletal, Julia hacked at the strong roots of dead yew bushes. My mother knocked on the window then ran outside. Panting, Julia looked up at her. She lifted the back of her wrist to her forehead and pushed aside a strand of hair. She gripped the shovel and said, "Gotta cut back these roots or the lily-of-the-valley will die. You leave me alone, now, and let me defeat something."

My mother would lay awake at night, consumed with thoughts of injustice. Julia was a good person and still she suffered. My mother thought about death. Heaven, Hell. Nothingness. She said fifty Hail Marys a day. Father Fitzpatrick lectured her on God's Plan, his sorrowful eyes magnified by the thick lenses of his glasses. The words provoked her. She dug her nails into her palms. Her mother said, "Try a rabbi." She found a synagogue in the yellow pages and walked five miles to it. The rabbi too talked about God's Plan. The united conviction like a pillow over my mother's face—she wanted a reason for my grandmother's pain. A reason.

43

The only person she could talk to was John. When JFK was assassinated, John wept for days and my mother punched a classmate who said it was "no great loss." This time, the nuns didn't punish, and when she told John, he stared in awe and called her his hero. They spent their free time together, going to movies, walking to and from the library, talking about boys. Sometimes they climbed out their respective windows and met in the middle of the night at the public school. They sat with their backs against the wall and watched the sky in silence. After years, there was one brick, close to the front door, with a dark black line through it, from John scraping out his cigarettes.

In 1964, when Julia entered a mild remission and Woody was home from college for the summer, they went as a family to Jones Beach. My mother took Somerset Maugham's *The Razor's Edge* from the bottom of the book pile. Her brother drove them in the Buick with his new license and itchy radio finger. Julia sat cranked back in the passenger seat and did a crossword puzzle, one pen in her hand, one tucked behind her ear. My grandfather, and Cousin John, sat in the back and thumb-wrestled over my mother's lap.

The aunts and uncles met them in the parking lot. Just like that, seventeen Irish-Catholics collecting towels and loved ones from a Buick. They planted the beach umbrella close to the shoreline. My grandfather built sand pillows then spread out the towels, kneeling on their flapping edges. At the edge of Long Island, the sky opened up. Waves sizzled over shells, a music like frying bacon. Salt. Seaweed. The horizon in shades of blue. Every now and then, a flush of cold wave swallowed their toes then retreated, leaving a bubbly trail in the sand.

My mother lay there, steeping in the sun, absorbing *The Razor's Edge*, her white legs swaddled in a towel. She identified with the war-scarred Larry Darrell, looking for answers, living with a yogi in India, seeing his past life in a candle. She read to the high-up drone of airplanes. Waves foamed over seagull tracks like trails of tiny kites. The hilarious syncopation of Uncle Jimmy's hiccups. Julia ashing at will: "All the beach's an ashtray." The uncles and Woody tossed a football back and

44

forth, skimming purposefully close to John, who was stretched out on a towel. The surf slammed and groaned. The tight pinch of sunburn across her nose. The dark shape of clouds over the ocean. This was the landscape of my mother's revelation. She read and felt the top of her head lifting away.

The concept of past lives was a comfort. What was the reason for her mother's suffering? She must have done something in a past life. There was justice in that, an Old World kind of justice. In a customized Irish-Catholic way, it made sense.

When everyone got up to swim, they left my mother reading, now shaded by a hat. The ocean heaved and broke upon itself like slabs of granite. She was so engrossed she didn't notice the waves snaking up, and when it was too late, she chose to save her book from the sea. The sandwiches were ruined. The towels soaked. The uncles scolded and teased her, "We can't live on words, Sheila. Some of us need actual food." Julia threw back her head and laughed.

She read *Siddhartha* at fifteen and found solace in the Buddha's words: "Life is suffering." Now that was an answer. Why? Because life is suffering. She said it to herself a hundred times a day: Life is suffering. She did not say it with doom or gloom; she said it matter-of-factly: Life is suffering. She read *The Tibetan Book of the Dead* and *The Eightfold Path. The Bhagavad Gita. The Ramayana. The Koran.* She read to understand, to find a place for her mother's agony, to hold up her religion against others, dogmatically. She took copious notes in margins, in pencil, and spent hours erasing before returning library books. She starched and ironed the family's clothes, cleaned the house, cooked three meals a day, went to high school, emptied ashtrays, learned to drive, babysat the neighborhood children, and became a self-educated expert in East Asia and India by the time she was sixteen.

In late 1964, she bought her first pair of blue jeans and ironed a pleat. John laughed till his freckles disappeared in his flushed cheeks, "That's the whole point of jeans, Sheila. You don't have to iron them."

"Well, at least I'm not ironing my underwear and sheets," she

45

snapped. "You know I can't abide a wrinkled cloth." She was disciplined, austere. She picked small, careful indulgences and had a fantasy of living as a cloistered nun. Books and a broom in a cell with one window. Her face changed, radiated light, when a smile cracked across it. The sudden beauty of an unlocked gate.

—∽—

When my mother turned seventeen, the World's Fair came to Queens. Its theme: Peace Through Understanding. The year of Vietnam, Johnson's War on Poverty, 25,000 marching from Selma to Montgomery, Charlie Brown on the cover of *Time*. My mother stuck a "Dissent Is Patriotic" pin through her purse-strap, and when *Dr. Zhivago* hit movie theaters, she fell hard for Omar Sharif.

Robert Moses, urban planner, designed and hosted the World's Fair. The Sullivans bore a grudge against him over the demolition of Coney Island and, later, the fact that he refused to name the Triboro Bridge after Bobby Kennedy. The family felt it anti-Irish-Catholic, to say nothing of stupid. But worst of all was Moses moving the Brooklyn Dodgers to California. The newly built Shea Stadium only mollified them slightly. The Sullivans would never support the Yankees. When the Dodgers left, there was nothing to do but turn into a Mets fan.

My grandfather brought my mother to the World's Fair the day after it opened. April 22, a spring day, bursting with madness and hope. Croci, daffodils, edging the pavement in purple and yellow. The trees swayed with soft green buds. My mother and grandfather parked the Buick and squinted through the half-mile lot, brilliant with the reflections of cars.

They wanted to see the old Feltman's Carousel first, removed from Coney Island when it was decided the Astrotower would make more money. All the Sullivans had gone to Coney Island on weekends in the 30s and 40s, when it cost a nickel to take the subway from the city. And my mother, Woody, and John had gone in the 50s, walking fast-footed over the splintery boardwalk, squealing when they accidentally stepped on the big bronze nail heads burning in the sun. My mother loved the stutter of the Ferris wheel, the briny smell of vinegar fries, the foaming surf bobbing with cans and sodden magazines. She and John watched the painted carousel horses, rearing in space, tiny light bulbs embedded in their saddles. The heavy up and down motion. The drift through time.

And now here was Feltman's Carousel, at the World's Fair. Even the misspelled sign was revived: CAROUSELL. A striped pink, blue, and white canopy covered the ride and matched the umbrellas shading the picnic tables. Pigeons rose from the pavement and flew between strings of incandescent bulbs.

As they walked, my mother felt like a buoy, lonely in the growing darkness. She felt old. She hunched her shoulders and moved closer to her father. They browsed the Transportation Area, thick with crowds staring up at the Sinclair Dinoland. Sparklers in the hands of children spat and glittered. A Brontosaurus, seventy feet long, twenty feet high, its head swinging back and forth. Next to it, a five-ton T-rex and Triceratops. My grandfather wondered aloud why Sinclair was so taken with dinosaurs. My mother said, "Daddy, it's an oil refining company. Oil comes from dinosaur bones." He saw her intelligence then, a mobile thing on her face. The way she made connections, understood the world around her, in context. He was proud of her but irritated by her tone. "Nobody likes a smart aleck," he said. "Just because you know things don't make you better than anyone else." She stuck her chin out, defiant. "Doesn't, Daddy. Not don't." He turned his back on her and she walked behind him, hurt. Then she ran forward and grabbed his hand. He squeezed her fingers, forgiving.

They passed a row of sleek metal huts, Bell's new touch-tone dialing system, and they used the showcased speakerphone to call Julia. My mother took a deep breath and listed everything they'd seen, talking fast, her words smearing to fit into a dollar of time. She kept wringing her hands; it felt strange to not hold a receiver.

Julia, wheezing, said, "Sheila. You'll be the first. Girl. To go. To college. With that mind. And the way you love to boss people around. You're meant to be. A teacher." My mother flushed with pleasure. Then the line went dead.

At the India Pavilion, she admired the look of black braids, the casual, crisp way women adjusted the cloths that kept their breasts covered. The shocking peek of a brown belly. She had read in *Newsday* that the warring nations of India and Pakistan were to have their pavilions placed a mile apart at the Fair to avoid any problems. She noted Indira Gandhi's careful words suggesting increased tensions between the two countries.

My grandfather tried to keep up but eventually sat down beside a rug exhibit to have a nap. My mother browsed with deliberation. The woman working the sari stall showed her how to wear one. My mother practiced three times and bought a shimmery green sari and a matching set of green tin bangles. She felt kindled. Her books flashed in her mind like fireworks. Her chest burned with a derelict love.

When she shook my grandfather awake he looked at her curiously and asked, "Why India?" She said, "It makes more sense to me." He laughed and shrugged.

At home, she modeled the green sari for Julia, who lit a cigarette, shuddered, and said, "What is it, for God's sake, a tablecloth?" My mother twirled around, "Isn't it beautiful?" Julia blew smoke out her nose in two long lines, a crashing contrail, and said, "What would the nuns think?" My mother shot back, "I'm a free-thinker, like you." Julia ashed delicately into the Stork Club tray Uncle Jimmy had lifted from work. A sudden knowledge sharpened her gaunt face. Her voice took on a tone of prophecy: "You're going to go there someday, aren't you. You'll marry one of them."

My mother went four more times to the World's Fair. Twice with my grandfather and twice with Cousin John. Each time, she spent at least three hours in the India Pavilion. She saved money from babysitting and bought Julia a Rajasthani necklace and bracelet. I used to play fancy dress up with them as a child.

48

In 1939, my grandfather had escorted his young wife to the World's Fair at the Grand Concourse. In 1964, he took my mother to Queens. Throughout the 80s and 90s, he and I went to Mets games at Shea Stadium, hollering for Gary Carter, Darryl Strawberry, Mookie Wilson. Filling out scorecards, stuffing peanuts and popcorn into our mouths. Stomping and clapping and screeching "Damnation" at every foul ball, me thinking we were saying "Damn Nation," and wondering why we were mad at the country. After the game, as we waited in traffic to exit the parking lot, we'd look over at Atlas shouldering his steel globe, the pink and orange Long Island sky shining through the open bars. My grandfather chucked his chin toward it. "World's Fair 64–65," he always said. "Your mother loved that."

—⁂—

They buried Julia at Holy Rood Cemetery on Route 110, beneath a pink granite stone lit by the erratic flicker of a gas station sign. Then they held a three-day Irish wake at the Hicksville house. Cars crammed the neighborhood; plates of food came and went. Fiddlers and whiskey, wild laughing, wild stories. My mother went to her room to lie down, sorrow gusting through her. She crawled under the covers just to feel weighted down and wept a terrible, certain, immobile weeping. Her brother came running, saying Uncle Billy, John's father, had put his hands on Aunt Lillian, and it wasn't the first time either. She wiped her face and got out of bed.

The uncles, drunk, grieving, dragged Billy outside. The family, dozens of Sullivans and a handful of Kents, stood on the front lawn watching as they beat him. The neighbors didn't bother to call the police because the police were Irish, too, and would have understood.

The sun set on the Sullivan men taking turns holding and punching Uncle Billy. His face as red and contorted as something newly born. The bloom of big city lights tinged the clouds to the west. The women gathered the children, sent them down the street with burlap sacks to Van Sise Farm. The potatoes and lima beans had just been harvested and the neighborhood was invited to glean remainders. Aunt Lillian and my mother got out the two biggest pots, the ones Julia had called the head-boilers. When the children returned, the men were still beating Uncle Billy on the lawn. The children dragged the bulging sacks of vegetables past the bloodshed and shelled the lima beans right into the pot.

Finally, the uncles dragged Billy inside and cleaned him up. They propped him on the couch and the women fixed him ice packs and whiskey and a plate of food, though his mouth was too swollen to open. It was understood, if he touched Lillian again, he would be killed. Nothing was forgotten but all was forgiven. Family was family.

My mother went back to her room. John found her there, weeping. She said, "Mommy wouldn't have let them fight." John arranged a white pillowcase over his head like a wimple and quietly sang, "How Do You Solve a Problem Like Maria?" He sang until my mother stopped crying and began to laugh. He said, "First Dr. King, then Bobby, then Julia. 1968 hasn't been a good year."

They ran the old home movies against the kitchen wall. My mother held a wet washcloth to Uncle Jimmy's bloody knuckles. Her father fell to his knees in grief. She leaned her head on John's shoulder. She was a Sullivan. They swapped miracles and sang "Scarlet Ribbons." The aunts and uncles filled the living room sofa and chairs, their eyes fixed on the Sacred Heart hung on the wall.

—⁙—

Until I was twenty-one, my parents told the story of how they met this way: in 1971, Cousin John was in nursing school and had a diabetic episode. The hospital put him in a bed overnight to make sure he was okay. My mother went to visit him and while she was sitting in the waiting room, my father, an intern, walked by.

On the day of my college graduation, I asked my father to tell the story again. He looked at me then said, "Ask Mommy."

I did, and the story changed:

50

John had a bad back, juvenile osteoporosis. That hump, always there, even when he was a kid. They called him The Hunchback of Notre Dame 'cause he was Irish. All of us have bad backs. Bursitis, scoliosis, osteoporosis. You name it. Well, John was in nursing school at Glen Cove Community Hospital. A doctor there gave him pills for his pain. First time in his life he got relief. He became a nurse partly 'cause he liked to help people and partly 'cause it was easier to get pills.

He came out to me when he was fifteen years old; only person in the world he told. You know how the family is. Staunch Catholics. We'd gone sledding and were at the bottom of the sump. Can't find a hill on Long Island unless you're in a sump. We'd fallen off the Flying Saucer he insisted we ride together. I'd carried it all the way from the house. I always did what he wanted 'cause he was younger than me. It was my brother's sled and believe you me, he'd check it for dents when I got back. So John and I had fallen off and were lying there in the snow. We were laughing but I was a little mad 'cause I had snow up my back and we'd scraped down to mud so I'd have to waste time later washing my coat. He said, "Sheila, I'm gay," and started to cry. He was hysterical. Truly hysterical. I said, "John, I know." He said, "Do you hate me?" I said, "I love you, Eejit." We called each other Eejit, the Irish way, back then. He sat smoking cigarettes and I held his other hand and we looked at the trees. I had given him my red nail polish earlier that day. I never used it, too busy taking care of my family and cleaning toilets at Tobay Beach to sit around painting my fingernails. My hands always smelled like bleach. Bleach and starch. John had painted first my mother's fingernails, then his own, sitting at the kitchen table, the two of them smoking while I did the week's ironing. She was too sick to do anything then. Could barely lift the cigarette to her mouth. John's nail polish was chipped from where he'd tried to flake it off so his father wouldn't see it and kick the shit out of him. We bought some remover after we left the sump.

One time when John was in nursing school, he made me go with him to this gay bar in Locust Valley, only gay bar on Long Island at the time. Called the Farquar. He wanted me to go with him in his car but I had one of my feelings and said no, I'd follow him in my own car. Well, the Farquar was in a bad part of town. Across from a grown-over lot and a falling-down church. Someone had spray-painted a white cross on the side of it. The bar still had Christmas lights up, even though it was spring. One of those balmy nights on the Island. Salty rain. Felt like it'd come in right off the ocean and skipped the clouds. John was ahead of me in his car, one hand holding a cigarette out the window. I could tell he was already dancing from the way his head bobbed. He took the Northern State and I turned on behind him. Woulda been faster to take the LIE but we both loved the trees on the Parkway and the mist floating around the streetlights. That night, he met his first boyfriend. I can't remember his name, but he was in his thirties and was a social worker. They were together about a year. I never liked him. He had five earrings in his left ear. I'd never seen that before. Wasn't any ear left with all those earrings. One gold cross, two gold studs, two gold hoops. God gave us a certain amount of holes. Why make more? The ones we got cause enough trouble as is. If I hadn't had my own car that night, John woulda kept me out till five in the morning while they hung all over each other dancing to Dolly Parton and Diana Ross and Barbra Streisand and all those other ambitious women gay men love. John never cared when I had work or school the next day. He'd keep me up all night long. And he was always late for everything. Drove me crazy. You know me. Call me anything but late for dinner.

For six years, I was the only one in the family who knew John was gay, although how they didn't know is beyond me. He dressed like Elton John. Same glasses and everything. Tight little bell-bottoms, always swishing around. But they didn't seem to know, or they didn't want to know. When I was twenty-four and John twenty-one, he decided to come out to the whole family. Every night on the phone I'd say, "Did you do it?" And he'd say "Not yet," and go into some elaborate story. Even when you were gutsy fighting Irish, like John, it wasn't an easy thing to do. Especially not in those days. Especially not to a family of Hell's Kitchen Irish-Catholics. Holy Mary Mother of God. What a nightmare. So John had a party one night. He invited all the nurses from his program and me. At first, the party was fun but then everybody got drunk and started doing those drugs they did back then. I always told John he'd be reincarnated as a snake 'cause of the drugs he took. I didn't like the drinking and drugging. I was working two jobs to get myself an education. I'd lost my mother. My brother *was getting shipped out to Vietnam. So when they got stupid I went into John's roommate's room to sleep. I had to get up the next morning and go to work. About eleven o'clock at night, this girl, a nurse that everybody called The Mouse, woke me up. She was screaming, "John's killed himself; John's killed himself!" I got up and followed her into John's room. He was lying on the bed. Couldn't see his chest moving. At all. The Mouse took his pulse. Said it was barely there. She went to call an ambulance. John looked dead. So flat and still. I started screaming. He'd taken the wooden cross from the wall behind his bed and was holding it in his hands. There was a note under the cross. I pulled it out and read it: "Dear Mom and Dad, I'm sorry. I'm gay. I can't stand the shame. I've seen a priest and there's nothing I can do." I'll never forget it. There was a bottle of pills next to his bed. He'd taken every one of the pills his doctor had given him for back pain. It was all very dramatic, all very John. I left the room to find the others. They'd left. Gone. Just like that. So I sat next to him. Patted his face. Said his name. Tried to keep him alive. At first they wouldn't let me on the ambulance with him. I said, "I'm his cousin, get out of my way." They kept asking me what he'd taken. I'd given them the bottle of pills and told them he'd been drinking. I didn't tell them he'd been doing drugs in case he got in trouble. John was unconscious, like a vegetable. They kept saying he was dying. When we got to the hospital, I stayed in the room while they pumped his stomach. He looked so flat and tiny. Skin was yellow. Eyes moving in weird jerky circles behind his lids. I was so scared. And for the first time I was glad my mother was dead so she wouldn't have to see him like that. Woulda killed her. She and John adored each other. Well, someone called his parents. And in they come, looking self-righteous and useless. I gave them the note. They read it and said it was all my fault, that I should have told them he was gay, they would have taken him to a whorehouse. I said, "What good would that do? He's gay, just leave him alone." Uncle Billy said I was disgusting, that I should be ashamed of myself. Now that's the pot calling the kettle black. I never talked to the son-of-a-bitch ever again. Never. He's still alive and if I ever see him, no words will cross these lips of mine.*

When John's parents got there, I wasn't allowed in the room anymore. I went and sat in the ICU waiting room. Green chairs. Hard plastic. Ugly as sin.

Had my Chinese workbook in my purse. I took it out and started studying. Too much work to be done to sit around crying, but I couldn't stop my cheeks from vibrating like I was riding a bike over a bumpy road or something. I was heart-broken over John. And I was pissed off. Pissed off at his asshole father. Pissed off at his friends. Pissed off at the Church. Pissed off that my mother was dead and I was cleaning toilets and my brother was going to war and my father was up to his ears in medical bills and my cousin had just tried to off himself.

John had told me about two Indian doctors at Glen Cove. One guy from Guyana, the other from Bombay. They both always signed up for overtime. Said they were pitiful, stringy guys, working themselves to death. John never had a kind word for foreigners. I said they were probably sending money back home to their families and trying to a make a living. I was right. They were both starting from scratch. One from Guyana had a wife and kid so the other one, from Bombay, covered his extra shifts. They said he was crazy, one from Bombay. Everybody called him the Hospital Ghost 'cause he never left and walked light on his feet and scared people when he came up behind them. He'd work double shifts three weeks in a row, take one day off, then come back again. Sometimes they put two chairs together, pushed him down on them and slid him under the nurse's station so no one could see him and he'd sleep a few minutes. John said he was always unshaven. Thin as a rail. Didn't seem to eat or sleep. Just worked like a dog. John had told him I said he'd be reborn as a snake for doing all those drugs and this son-of-a-bitch doctor said, "You can't be reborn beneath the human station." So John would say I was wrong, that he could keep doing drugs 'cause a real Indian had told him he wouldn't be reborn as a snake. So there I am, sitting in the ICU waiting room, grieving for my cousin who's just killed himself, and in walks this unshaven Indian in a Dr. Kildare intern jacket. And he stares at me. Told me later all he saw was a pretty girl with long brown hair reading what looked to him, at first glance, to be Hindi. He came right up next to me, looked down at my book. I snapped it closed. He said, "What are you doing?" I said, "What does it look like I'm doing? I'm studying Chinese." I opened the book and kept reading. He didn't go away. So I said, "I bet you're the doctor who told my cousin John he couldn't be reborn as anything less than a human. Well, let me tell you something about

Hinduism . . ." and gave him a good lecture. He just stood there listening, sometimes interrupting me. He might have been a Indian but he hadn't read anything about the religion he'd been born into. All the nurses and doctors kept coming in and talking to me 'cause everybody knew John. Your father never left. Just kept standing there. It turned April 1, 1971 while we were talking. He told me his Mataji said it was foretold in his horoscope he'd meet the woman he'd marry on April 1, 1971. Later he told me Mataji also said the woman would have a funny nose. You know me and my sinuses. Well, he said he was going on a break, that he lived across the street in medical student housing, that I looked tired, why didn't I come back to his place, someone would call him if anything happened with John. So I did. I went over there with him and when he opened the door, Jesus, Mary, and Joseph, the smell. It was terrible. I took one look at his bathroom and started cleaning. God, I hate a dirty bathroom. Looked like he was growing penicillin in the tub. Holy Mary Mother of God, it was filthy. And the dishes, stacked ceiling high in the sink. Well, I couldn't stand it. Man had no money, worked around the clock trying to help people. He was far from home, too. You know, the only doctor my mother ever liked was an Indian at Long Island College Hospital in Brooklyn. She'd call him a heathen when he left the room but she trusted him. Well, I cleaned. Scrubbed everything in the apartment till it sparkled. Got down on my hands and knees, too, and did the kitchen floor in jig time. Well, if you're gonna do something. I cleaned till four in the morning and he followed me around, talking, handing me little cups of tea. I cleaned till that entire apartment was Virgin Mary immaculate. I told him if nothing else, he should keep his apartment clean so he didn't give his people a bad name. People say Indians are dirty, you know, I told him. So you can't be. I told him the Sullivans might have been poor but they kept a spotless house. No one could call them dirty Irish and have it be true. He went in the bathroom and took off his glasses and washed his face. I stood next to him, talking. Saw those dents at the sides of his nose. Deep and red from his heavy glasses. Thick as Coke bottles, they were. He reached for the towel with those long hands of his. I liked his nose. And that shiny black hair. Could tell he kept his own counsel. And he wasn't afraid of a mouthy broad like me. He reminded me of Omar Sharif.

Well, we went back over to the hospital and he sat with me in the waiting room. They said John was probably going to live. That's when I started crying. When I knew he'd live. My hands stank of bleach even more than usual from cleaning your father's apartment. I was so tired. I knew my right eye was going cross-eyed like it does. Your father asked me out on a date to see that movie, The Hospital. I shoulda known right then he'd be married to his work. Inviting me to The Hospital, for God's sake, and him spending every waking minute in one.

John stayed in Glen Cove a week. When they decided he didn't have brain damage, they sent him to the King's Park nuthouse. His parents kept him there a month. I went to see him every day. There was one guy who walked around wearing two pairs of pants. Poor bastard didn't remember putting on the first pair so he'd put on another. Musta had Alzheimer's or something. John hated it there. Said he wished he'd finished himself off so he didn't have to live with a bunch of crazies. They made him talk to social workers, priests, you name it. Every day, for hours. Finally, they just gave up. He was gay. That was that. They let him out. He went back to nursing school and loving men. His parents stopped talking to him. Nobody but me and my father and Aunt Jo stood by him. Divide and conquer, like the British. That's what the family did. I said, John, this is their problem, not yours. You're just being who you are. You're not doing anything wrong. He'd cry and cry. He was so unhappy. We'd always been a close family. Fighting and loving hard, the Irish way. I hated to see him suffer like that. He never hurt anybody but himself. Never.

You know I was dusting downstairs the other day and I found that little white bell, remember it? Had it with me in my purse, the day John committed suicide. Yeah, I know he didn't commit suicide, I was there, remember? He didn't die, but after that night, he was a new man. Killed the old John. The one that was afraid. Couple years later he moved out to San Francisco. Met Jim. You want to hear the story or not? Well then shut your mouth. I'd been paid from the beach that morning, for cleaning the Godforsaken toilets. There was less work to do in the cold months. You can't imagine what it was like in summer. Every woman who went into those bathrooms dropped a little pile of sand from the crotch of her bathing suit. Pissed all over the seats, too. Especially those North Shore women. Rich as Croesus. They'd stand on line staring at me while

I mopped, like, Hurry up bitch, get it done. *There's nothing more futile than cleaning sand at a beach. Well, there was less work in winter, at least. And I'd gone straight from Tobay to Hofstra. Paid my tuition. Gassed up the car. Had a little money left over. Right there in my pocket. Decided to go to Macy's and look at the nice stuff. I saw that little bell in the Homewares Department and knew my mother would love it. She had been dead two years. But she woulda loved it. It was like something from the top of a wedding cake. White bone china. Shaped like Scarlett O'Hara. Pink and blue flowers at the top. Little white clapper inside. It was something. I bought it for my mother. Had it with me all that night at the hospital with John. Next day, I drove home from Glen Cove and put the bell on the mantle. When Daddy saw it he said, "Wouldn't your mother love that?" He stood there looking at it for a long time. I tell you. Men like your grandfather are scarcer than hen's teeth.*

Your father took me to Montauk on our second date. We bought that towel you like so much, the one with the seagulls. It was expensive so we split it. He said we could share it so I knew I'd see him again. He said my eyes were as blue as water on maps. We went out to the Big Duckie, too. Your father liked that big wooden duck. Made him laugh. Long Island was still all farms back then. Farms and fishermen and hard-working Jews. Good quiet place.

A little while after we started dating, your father and I took the train to the City so I could introduce him to Uncle Jimmy. I had a key to his apartment so we let ourselves in. I remember there was a stew in a Crockpot on the counter and the whole place smelled like garlic. Jimmy was the only man I knew in those days who used garlic in his cooking. It was something he'd picked up in Italy when he was a cook in the navy. Well, Jimmy was sitting on the couch, drunk. He took one look at your father and went red in the face and scalp. He pulled me into the bedroom and said I had to stop seeing your father. He said it wasn't right, wasn't natural. I tried to reason with him. I said I loved your father, and that your grandfather and uncle did, too. I said people used to treat us bad for no reason, how can you do this to someone else? But Jimmy wouldn't listen. He staggered around, saying awful things. When he started opening dresser drawers and hurling clothes on the bed, I left the room and took your father's hand and we walked out of there. I never saw Jimmy again. He didn't call to apologize and he didn't stop by to see us, not even after we were married and you were born. It broke my heart, losing him.

That hospital. Glen Cove Community. One fine day, about two years after we had our first date, your father called me up and said he had a pain between his bellybutton and hip. "In McBurney's Point." I said, "Sounds like a good place for a picnic." His appendix was about to burst. Said he was gonna hang up the phone, walk across the street to the ER, and ask Dr. Lewis to operate. Well, I rushed over. Skipped class. Traffic was terrible. Took me forever. When I got to the hospital, I said, "I'm here to see Dr. Vaswani, his appendix burst." All the nurses went silent. They said, "Who are you?" I said, "I'm his girlfriend." They all looked at each other. One of them took me by the arm into a back room and drew a curtain. She said, "Keep your voice down. I'm sorry to tell you the doctor died last night." I said, "That's impossible, I just talked to him an hour ago." All the other nurses came behind the curtain and crowded around. I said, "He's not dead. I spoke to him." They looked at each other and then at me like I was ranting and raving, out of my mind with grief. I said, "I'm telling you, I just talked to him; he's not dead; check the papers and tell me what room he's in." I was getting hysterical. It was all so surreal. Finally someone asked me to write his name down. All those foreign names sounded alike to them. Turned out a Dr. Viviani, an Italian guy, had died the night before. He was married so when I said I was his girlfriend, they thought he had a little something on the side. So for twenty minutes there, I thought your father was dead. Feel? How did it make me feel? What a stupid question. How do you think it made me feel? I loved the son-of-a-bitch.

—∞—

My parents told me of the Vaswanis, the Sullivans. They told stories as an act of love, as resurrection. Something to be turned to in a time of need.

Sometimes, as a child, I would lie awake thinking about that fight on the day of my grandmother's funeral. I had lived with my parents, grandfather, and Uncle Woody, in that Hicksville house for two years, although I was a baby and don't remember it. But I have breathed that air and I learned to walk on those floors. It hurt me to think that Uncle Billy's sins could be forgiven, but ours and John's could not. The sin of difference, of going outside your own kind, worse than molestation on the day of a funeral.

By the time I was born, most of the Sullivans were dead from hard, full living. The ones that remained were a generation away from Hell's Kitchen and always seemed vaguely disapproving of my father and me, of my mother and her peculiar choices. She always said, "Blood is thicker than water," but it seemed to me that my mother's blood had deserted her.

My father, a refugee, could never go back to Sindh: Pakistan did not let Sindhis re-enter for fear of land claims. My father said, "Homeland is in the body," and, "Land is in the blood."

When I was a child, I imagined dirt running in my veins, clotting thick, sweeping around my bones and sinew. My favorite toy was The

Visible Woman. I twisted and punched her skeleton and organs out of a plastic rack, painted them, and placed each in the proper spot in her body cavity. I glued her shut, but she broke soon after. So I filled her with dirt, dug a shallow trench, and buried her in the same earth that filled her guts.

WHAT FALLS BETWEEN

April 24, 1980. 4 AM. The neighbor's dog barks a greeting. She quivers, snuffles the foreign dust of our suitcase and escorts us from the car to the house, nearly tripping my mother, who whisper-hisses, "Go home, Coco. It's too late for shenanigans."

In the darkness, I smell lilacs. When we left Long Island, it was Christmas. Now, it is spring. At the door, we step out of our shoes and lean our rolling suitcase against the kitchen table. My father, with his easy grace, whisks down the hallway in slippers, whistling. Within moments, he raises the heat and changes into shorts. A steaming cup of tea on a tray balanced in his right hand. He sneezes and announces, "Temperature change." From India to the United States, the body adjusts.

In his room at the back of the house, my grandfather sleeps beneath a knotted green rosary and a carved wooden plaque: MAY YOU BE IN HEAVEN A HALF AN HOUR BEFORE THE DEVIL KNOWS YOU'RE DEAD. A half drunk glass of whiskey perched on the edge of his bedside table.

My mother and I sit on the floor of the tiny laundry room, plucking clothes from the suitcase. She is sunburned; I am dark brown. We empty pockets, make a teetering pile of coins, passports, hankies. In the easy electric light, we shake out stiff blouses and long skirts smelling of clay. They have been washed in rivers, beaten against rocks, for the past four months. There is the clank of buttons and zippers tossing in the dryer.

This is the house where the dryer has a broken timer. It tumbles endlessly and burns up socks. Cacti line the top. Nestled in ceramic pots, they thrive in the manufactured heat. To every new house, the cacti move with us. Packed in boxes lined with newspapers, like broken birds found on the street.

The house hums with our displaced wakefulness. Time, the strange gift of exile. All our journeys end in a laundry room at 4 AM, windows blazing yellow into the surrounding darkness.

Outside, it begins to rain. Thunder rattles the windows. My mother and I stand at either end of a sheet, snap, once. Between us, it billows up, white hopeful arc.

—⚬⚬—

Each of my parents is a story to me. A country. My mother: America. My father: India.

As a family, we wandered. We had no *here*. Only there. And there. And there. Something would scratch inside us if we stayed more than three years in one place. By the time I was eighteen, we had lived in thirteen homes and traveled to twenty-five countries on doctor swaps and teaching tours. Wherever we went, my father said, "I am Sindhi." Wherever we went my mother was Irish-Catholic, said in one breath as if one did not exist without the other.

On our fourth move, from Hicksville, Long Island, to Jericho, Vermont, my grandfather did not come with us. But my grandmother Vaswani traveled from India to visit for two years.

—⚬⚬—

1978. Vermont. Miss Maureen, my teacher at the free preschool in the basement of St. Pius X, had a pair of brown shoes with small open circles at the toes that made her feet look like hooves.

When Miss Maureen wore those shoes, I loved to run away from her. She sounded like a teeny-tiny horse as she came clicking after me, wisps of blonde hair slipping from a strict ponytail that pulled the skin at her temples taut. Miss Maureen played the ukulele, and when it rained she drew back the curtains so we could watch the fog swallow the mountains. She drove a rusty blue Mercedes that smelled like fried chicken because it ran on a combination of diesel and restaurant grease. She called it "The Jimmy Carter Special" which always made my parents laugh.

Miss Maureen wore skirts with square pockets big enough for wooden blocks, and long-sleeved blouses with lacy, squat-collared ruffs. From her right sleeve, every day, dangled a pink plastic rosary. She was younger than my mother, but something old and lonely leaned in the slope of her shoulders. Even when the other teachers ate upstairs in the rectory, Miss Maureen unwrapped her thin turkey sandwich, stepped out of her peep-toe shoes, sank down onto a blue padded mat with her naked feet tucked up under her haunches, and had lunch with us children. She sat on the floor and laughed big. I adored her. We all did.

Miss Maureen said I was green. Olive green. She said I was green because of my Daddy who had been an American for only six months. She said green as if it was a neutral hue on the spectrum of human skin. When she said *green*, her voice sounded fenced like Mr. Raddick's goats. I could hear the goats early in the morning as they cracked heads. The sound carried over the mountain, crisp as a gunshot.

I did not understand the meaning of Miss Maureen's fenced voice, but I knew the sensation that rose in me, alert, was important. The feeling lifted a paw and sniffed the air, warily. The feeling did not intrude upon my love for Miss Maureen, but sat down right next to it.

Miss Maureen's fenced voice was something crouched and hidden, that she did not know had taken up residence inside her.

Her fenced voice, my wariness—the two belonged to each other.

—m—

When Miss Maureen said I was green, I felt she must be right.

I held my left wrist in my right hand, and, in this manner, took my left hand around the house as if it were not attached to me. I let it hang, limp, a dead weight. My right hand held my left hand up against green things—

the towel with a bleach stain my mother said was ruined, my father's I LOVE SCIENCE t-shirt, the cucumbers fat and pimpled in the garden.

My hand matched nothing green.

I sat outside in the green grass. Everything around me, alive, alive, and thrumming. The trees, the songs of sparrows, the fast-beating wings of flies. I looked at the stillness of the greened-over pond, teeming with unseen creatures, the top of the water rigid with algae. Three white-haired cows grazed near a white fence. A crop of red strawberries clung tight to runnels of dirt. Behind the garden, where the field turned long and weedy, two brown does nested side by side.

I thought about green beings. Lord Vishnu. The Wicked Witch of the West. My grandmother, Dadi, and I liked the Hulk and Kermit (for some reason, she called Kermit *ograi*, the Sindhi word for burp). Sometimes I pushed a sack of Basmati rice under my pant leg to look like Hulk muscles. I clawed at my shirt and roared a little. My grandmother cackled and clapped her hands. She didn't speak English and I didn't speak Sindhi, but we could still make each other laugh.

I went inside and opened the fridge stocked half with food, half with agar plasma plates. The cold tang of mustard wafted out. My daddy always said it was important to be thorough and scientific. I took the jar of olives that lived on the lowest shelf and sat on the floor. The jar sweated slick between my knees. It took four tries but I twisted off the cap and fished out an olive, using my pinkie to hook its gaping mouth.

I balanced the olive on top of my hand. It dripped like a wet seal.

We did not match.

I was brown. I was brown like my daddy whom my mother and I loved more than anything on God's green earth.

I became a Hoover and sucked out the red pimento. Then I put the olive, empty, back in the jar. It floated in the brine, a little lighter than the others.

For dinner, my mother made her customary salad. I followed her around the kitchen. When she took my olive out of the jar, I asked her how come that one she was holding didn't have any red inside. "Every olive's different," she said. She looked sad when she said it and I felt sorry for fooling her. I told her about Miss Maureen's shoes like hooves. She said, "Cloven. That's the word. Like goats and the devil. How a good Irish-Catholic girl can wear shoes like that is beyond me. Gives me the heebie-jeebies."

—⁓—

Once a week, my mother spread the Sports Pages of the *Green Mountain News* out on the kitchen floor, carefully overlapping the edges so no bit of wood showed through. She hated sports and was particular about a clean floor. She was an editor at the newspaper and when she pointed to articles she told stories about the people who had written them: Joan who had polio and wore a lift in one shoe; Felice who kept chickens and sold fresh eggs on Wednesdays; Bob with the framed picture of Julie Christie on his desk.

Every Friday night, my mother set her sneakers down on the names and bylines of her coworkers and slathered her shoes into a glaring whiteness. I loved the little bottle of polish with a sponge for a head. My mother squeezed its plastic sides and painted her sneakers everywhere but the soles. She let me sit next to her with her bottle of Wite-Out. "Sparingly," she warned. "Costs a pretty penny." I dipped the brush halfway into the bottle then swiped carefully across the newspaper, blotting out the words I could recognize.

When we finished polishing, we lined the windowsill in the kitchen with the obituaries and set my mother's sneakers to dry. Those Friday nights, summertime, we sat at the kitchen table and shucked corn from the garden, filling brown grocery bags with yellow silk and green skins, what my mother called refuse but what seemed to me the most interesting part. The wind cast the smell of shoe polish around the room and set the edges of the newspaper rustling. I wasn't strong enough to shuck more than one leaf of corn in each pull, but my mother could grit her teeth and do four at a time, and my father could do all of them at once and then snap off the extra length of stem with one hand. "Show-off," my mother always said, with pleasure, when he did that.

I loved how tightly the leaves wrapped around the corn. A strong skin, keeping it safe. I loved the sticky pale strings. I loved the way my mother announced mealtimes, screaming out, "It's feeding time at the zoo!" We made dinners of masala omlettes, mine and my father's and grandmother's packed with green chiles from the garden. My mother shaped leftover mashed potatoes into small round patties, added cumin and onion, and fried Sindhi *tiki*. We liked eating breakfast for dinner; we liked turning time upside down. My grandmother and I ate with our hands. My mother and father, with forks. It was okay to lean across the table for butter so long as you said, "Boardinghouse reach." For dessert, we had plates of salted and peppered cucumbers bathed in juice squirted from a plastic lemon with a green flip-up spout. Sometimes my daddy made banana splits and wore the peels over his ears to be funny. Sometimes he made a pie. He used the long, skinny rolling pin my grandmother had brought from Calcutta, and Dehradun wheat. He rolled out the pie crust as if it was *roti* then let me stab it with a fork to make heat vents.

Always, my mother sighed when she took her first bite, "Mother Mary and St. Bride. That's good pie." Always, my grandmother ate only the crust, with her fingers, eyeing the hot apple filling with disdain.

—m—

One Friday night, my mother sat at the kitchen table cutting coupons. She never used a scissor to cut coupons; instead, she folded the paper and ripped, carefully, along the crease. "We're going food-shopping," she said to me and my father, then, "Being alive is expensive, Neela Ashok." When she tied the laces of her sneakers, polished stiff and white, there was a quiet crunch, like the step of a cat on frozen grass.

She said only weirdos went to Grand Union late on Friday nights. She had polished her sneakers. It was Friday night, and it was late. Me, him, her.

I rode the front of the grocery cart, tracked a piece of tape flapping from the back wheel, and listened to my mother's sneakers squeaking against the tile floor. We rolled toward aisle four, on the hunt for tea in little bags. My father liked his tea loose and boiled with milk and *elachi*, but he had run out of Red Label and India was far away. My throat felt tight and I rubbed my nose with the flat of my hand. I worried I might have a nosebleed. My mother had turned the prevention of them into an act of dignity. "Keep your chin up. Look the world in the eye," she said. But I liked to look at little things down near my feet. A stone, a cricket. My head followed my eyes down, and then my nose gushed. This had been happening for about a month and my daddy said if it didn't stop soon, we'd have to do something.

He stood by the Tabasco sauce, cradling a stack of canned chickpeas. He grinned at me and said, "We need to find the Red Hot." I knew what the bottle looked like: FRANK'S in stocky letters and a picture of a red chili with a green stem.

When I spied the shelf of FRANK'S, I looked down and pointed. The tickle at the back of my throat bloomed. My nose gushed blood but it was my own and did not frighten me. It was warm against my chin and neck and smelled like carrots torn from the earth. I felt tired and sat down. My mother screamed. My father dropped the cans of chickpeas and picked me up. Spinning lights. An ambulance. Her face, his face, long and bright with fear. A rattling I thought was our bones but my father said was the rails of the metal stretcher. It felt strange to be the only one lying down.

When we got to the hospital, a doctor in a white paper hat, like Nehru, like the freckled boy on the Kentucky Fried Chicken billboard, stuck a hot poker up my nose. It stopped bleeding. I cried and my mother distracted me by telling me how to spell "cauterized."

69

It was morning when we got home from the hospital. The cows lowed invisible in the fog. My father lifted me out of the backseat. Dadi, my grandmother, waited at the front door, under the yellow light bulb caged in a white frosted circle. The light was on and seemed weak against the growing dawn. Bugs circled Dadi's head. She didn't brush them away. She had a great stillness in the face of bugs.

My father carried me into my room and arranged some pillows so I could sleep sitting up. My mother pulled the curtains closed. Through the space where the curtains did not quite meet I saw a limb of the apple tree. I shivered and held my arms out, watching my skin erupt into sharp little magic points. I breathed through my mouth, my nostrils bulging from the gauze packed inside them. The doctor and my daddy agreed I would not be able to speak for at least a week. I pretended I had taken a vow of silence, like Vishwamitra. I pretended my silence was a language with a grammar of its own.

My daddy let me wear his National Guard boots on my hands. We both loved those boots. He had joined the National Guard the day after he was sworn in as an American citizen. He moved the fishbowl from the window to the little table by my bed so I could watch Sonali the goldfish swim round and round. He gave me his spare stethoscope and said if I felt better later, I could go outside and listen to the heartbeats of trees. I clapped the soles of his boots together.

It was Saturday so only my daddy had to go to work. He left early to stop at the Grand Union and buy the groceries we'd left stacked in the cart. After he was gone, I remembered the bottle of FRANK'S. I hadn't put it in the cart. I had only reached for it.

—⚍—

We always laughed about FRANK'S and called it Daddy's Sauce, because of the day on the hospital elevator. My mother and I had gone to visit. The doors opened and three doctors in white coats stepped aboard. "Hey there, Frank," they said to my father, and kept talking to each other.

70

My mother said, "Ashok, who the hell is Frank?" He shrugged and shot my mother a look. She pressed her lips into a single line. "Excuse me," she said, and tapped one doctor on the shoulder until they all stopped talking. The expression of shock made their faces look alike. They stared at my mother as if she were crass, terrifying. She said, "The man's name is Ashok. It's not hard. Ashok. Rhymes with Coke." We rode up three floors in silence. After the doctors got off the elevator, my mother said savagely to my father, "You can't let them call you that. It's not your name. You have to demand they say it right. They're not going to do it on their own." My father said, "Yeah, yeah, it's okay, it's okay." He was angrier at my mother than the doctors. She was angry with him and the doctors both.

Every time my mother uttered her last name to a stranger, she would say: "It's like the song," (here she would sing), 'Way down upon the Swanee River' (here she would stop singing). Swanee River with a VA in front of it. Va-Swanee. Get it? Got it? Good."

In our family, it was quietly understood that my mother could do some things with more safety than my father. She had Americanness. Whiteness. Pretty femaleness. We would put her up to things together. Making dentist appointments, asking for a clean fork in a restaurant, arguing with Sears about a broken fridge. She was native, a translator, a buffer. Allowed to complain and make demands and be indignant. She was acceptable.

Standing next to me or my father, she became strange. But, even then, of the three of us, she was the most native and so went first through most doors. In that initial moment, she was invisible, looking like everyone else in the room. But when my father, grandmother, and I walked in, the air changed—vibrated with questions, judgments, curiosity, disgust, delight. Anything but neutrality.

We formed a triangle of foreignness. Because of my father, my mother was a foreigner to her own people. Because of my mother, my father was a foreigner to his own people. And I was both of them, a foreigner to everyone except myself. I developed an ability to hold two things in my

71

mind at once. Two feelings, two ideas, two languages. The in-between, inside me. Like two spotlights on a dark stage, coming together. And where they overlapped, it was brightest. It was easiest to see.

My mother sat on the edge of my bed and sang my favorite song—the alphabet. I liked that the alphabet could be sung in any key, like "Happy Birthday." My mother sang the alphabet like a dirge. I heard her grief, deep as the roots of turnips. I hummed a few notes along with her but then my throat hurt so I stopped. Dadi sat in a chair by the window. The white of her gauzy widow's sari matched the white of my polyester curtains. She tapped her hand against her thigh to keep the beat. If my mother looked up, Dadi stopped tapping and stared blankly out the window. She was mad at my mother for being American.

My father had written to Dadi in a translucent blue aerogram to say he was married and had a child. He had written in Hindi that his wife's name was Sheela. Sheela, an Indian name. He sent a plane ticket and my grandmother came, expecting a Sindhi daughter-in-law. For some reason, I always imagined the letter my father had written lost in the mail, my grandmother not knowing for years that my mother and I existed.

My mother handed me a slate, black and cold with a driftwood border. "You can't talk but you can write," she said. She plucked my daddy's boots from my hands. "No shoes on the bed," then drew lines in white chalk across the slate. She put letters between the lines. A, B, C, D. As she wrote in her wild, slashing way, the chalk clicked against the slate. Three times for the unbent limbs of A. Two clicks and a squeaky swoon for straight-backed B and its humps.

The curtains bellied and sagged with the wind and sometimes stuck to the screen where the mesh lay broken. I liked those jagged holes. They let the outside in. Once, a caterpillar had crawled from a limb of the apple tree through a hole in the screen and onto a piece of paper lying on my desk. I drew a woman's face on the paper, the caterpillar standing in for an eyebrow. When it inched away, the face had only one eyebrow.

Dadi knew it aggravated my mother when the curtains stuck to the screen but she did not stand up to free them. She hummed the alphabet and tapped her long hand against her knee.

"You do it now," my mother said. "Write. Keep practicing." The bed sighed as she stood up to free the curtains.

I wrote my favorite word: *and*. Plop *and* down between two words and bring them closer together. Sheila and Ashok. Elwood and Sita. County Kerry and Sindh. Guru Nanak and Jesus Christ. John and Jim. Lata Mangeshkar and Cat Stevens. Happy and sad and good and bad. To join things, even opposites, was as easy as writing the word *and*.

I practiced *and* in cursive. The fancy curves and arabesques. Letters, roped together. No space between them. No oceans or grudges or secrets. I could feel the shape of the scar in my nose, how it tilted up at the corners. I had squirmed under the hot tip of the poker and the movement arced the scar. I knew the length and width of the scar from the path of my pain. I liked the pain. It was mine. We belonged to each other. I kept breathing through my mouth. I kept mute. My mother read my face and eyes. Silently, I wrote. I liked that a written sentence had no accent. Written, words were just themselves.

I fell asleep in the shape of an S.

When I woke, my mother was gone and Dadi lay next to me in bed. She was tiny, like me, and we fit with each other. The doorbell rang. "*Nahin,*" Dadi said, and draped an arm over me. "*Eedhar terho.*" Stay here. She never answered the doorbell because she didn't speak English. When it rang, she hid in the bathroom. If I answered the door, she ran from the bathroom, shouting in Sindhi, swinging her *paloo* over her head in a graceful arc. Then she stood behind me, glaring, and shut the door in people's faces.

The doorbell rang again. We lay there, listening. Whoever it was, left.

We played our favorite game of numbers and words. She said *billie, chuha, kutta, hikka, ba, the,* ticking the words and numbers off the segments of her fingers. Everyone in my Indian family counted up to fourteen on one hand. Three slots on each finger, two on the thumb. "Wasted math," my father said when my mother counted one number per finger. It seemed to me Indian fingers held more numbers like Indian music held more notes. Dadi said, "Cat, mouse, dog, one, two, three," the words cramped and unfamiliar at the back of her mouth. She cackled after each word. English was funny nonsense, not as real a language as Sindhi or Hindi. I wrote in English on the slate. Dadi huddled next to me in bed and watched Sonali swimming round and round the fishbowl. Before I wiped the slate clean, I showed her my letters. She nodded. She could not read the words, but they were written by her *poto,* her granddaughter, and that made them good. I felt comforted by the quiet length of her body. We watched Sonali sweep her orange tail through the clarity of water. We were silent. Fish, grandmother, *poto.* Light leached palely through the curtains hanging in tandem at the window. Neither one of us fixed the curtains when they caught on the jagged screen. Sometimes we read. Me in English, Dadi in Sindhi. I read from left to right. She read from right to left. We turned our pages in opposite directions, our black eyes moving across the words backward, forward, in unison.

I ran my hand down the bumpy white of Dadi's long braid. I liked to lay it across my palm and feel its weight. Each strand, so light. Bound together, strong as rope. A chickadee alighted on the screen, the sound of its claws scratching quietly. It sang out and I watched its throat swell and sink around the sharp, clear notes. When it flew away, the screen rattled and I heard the bird's wings beat twice against the hot, thick air.

Sometimes we ran our hands over my Holly Hobbie wallpaper, slightly swollen with humidity, her profiled figure repeating over and over on the north wall. I traced the outline of one Holly Hobbie while Dadi traced another. We raced to see who could outline the quickest.

I liked that Holly Hobbie was faceless. All that could be seen of her profile was a huge brim of blue bonnet and a mass of reddish-brown curly hair. Not smooth hair like blonde Maryanne who lived across the street. But messy, raging curls. I loved the color of Holly Hobbie's hair. Reddish brown, like mine, like Brendan and Nieve's, who had a Chinese mother and Irish father. Reddish-brown like the little girl I saw once at the supermarket in Hicksville who had a black mother and white father. Holly Hobbie could be Black or Irish or Indian or Chinese. It was impossible to tell under that hair and bonnet. She was country, that was clear—her quilted smock, high-laced boots—but everything else about her remained ambiguous.

Dadi and I traced Holly Hobbies for a while. Then we watched the aging light of evening creep through the space between the curtains. I fell asleep again. When I woke up, I heard Dadi singing bhajans to herself as she shuffled down the hall. I heard the whine of the front door. Suddenly, through the crack in the curtains, I saw her long wrinkled hand reach up and cup an apple, bright red, hanging from a limb of the tree. I felt a wash of love for the apple attached to the hand of my grandmother.

She brought the apple indoors to me on a tray with a stack of Arrowroot *biscoots* leaned up against each other, and a sizzling glass of Coca-Cola on ice. My parents did not allow me to drink soda, but Dadi always snuck it to me. I held the apple, pressed its sun-warmed skin against my cheek. I sipped soda through a straw that kept bobbing up, propelled by bubbles. I wouldn't let it escape. I caught it between my teeth. The sweet soda broke over my tongue, wiggled against the roof of my mouth. There was no drink as alive as Coca-Cola.

I drew a picture of Sonali on the slate and wrote her name in Hindi and English underneath her portrait. I showed Dadi. She nodded and patted my hand. We shared the rest of the glass of soda, scudding the straw against the bottom of the glass, making the suctiony noises of air that always caused my mother to say, "Don't be crude, Neela Ashok." Then we sat silent and watched the sash of sunlight on my bed narrow into a thin yellow line. Dadi chucked her chin at the light and judiciously went to the kitchen. I heard running water, the squeak of a towel, the click of a glass settled next to others like it in the cabinet, and Dadi's little grunt as she pushed the empty soda can to the bottom of the garbage bag where it would not be found.

—⁓—

1982. East Northport, Long Island. My mother, thirty-four, a student teacher.

She was grading papers, red pen hovering over dates of war, treaty, global capital, when I asked what heathen meant.

She murmured: "Unbaptized."

I left her, climbed the tree out front that we called Mabel the Maple. Bare sticks stood black on the lawn. I looked down at the dogwood tree, stunted and shaking with starlings. Flapping, squawking, filling the naked branches like leaves. It seemed more bird than tree, as if it could lift off and fly away. I wrapped my arms around Mabel's trunk. A pale sun shot the air with heatless light.

Baptism. Such a small motion. Water dropped onto the head. I decided I would baptize myself. I didn't want to be Catholic. I just wanted to be rid of the word *heathen*. The way it hissed and bit.

I slid down Mabel. Trotted across the lawn. Opened the front door. I stood looking in at my mother hunched over student papers, her red pen scrawling. Cup of tea steaming by the stapler. I could tell her bursitis ached from the way she sat, as if tricking her shoulders. She said, without looking up, "Shut it tight."

76

I pulled my feet from my sneakers by stepping on the heels, something that made my mother mad, but she was looking down so I got away with it. "Take care of things and they'll last forever," she always said. The house, one-level, hummed with a concentrated quiet. The outside cold vented through the walls, casting a chill on the backs of my legs. I took ten steps into the kitchen and the flowing baseboard heat.

"If I put water on my head, will I be baptized?"

Startled, my mother laughed. The sound had peaks and valleys. She leaned back, withdrew a tissue from her sleeve, looked at me half-scornful, half-pitying: "It's not just water. It's a commitment. You'd have to go to Sunday school. You'd have to do Communion and be confirmed. You'd have to believe in the Creed." She was wearing one of my grandfather's flannel shirts, and, underneath, an iron-on t-shirt custom-made at the flea market: VIOLENCE IS NOT THE ANSWER on the front. MAHATMA GANDHI on the back.

I padded over to her in socked feet. I asked her what happened to heathens. She pushed the tissue back up her sleeve, set down her pen: "You go to Limbo. Heathens get off easy. Just denied the Eternal Vision. Catholics go to Purgatory. It's hot and horrible there, full of suffering. But that's only what Catholics believe. For all I know, the dead feed earthworms, and nothing more or less than that happens." She tapped my arm, "Limbo's okay. Just don't think about it anymore." She picked up her pen.

Limbo was the only thing she ever told me not to think about; she told me to think about everything.

She went back to marking papers, her mouth perched on the rim of her cup. She breathed into the tea to cool each sip. I stayed, silent, next to her. I thought about missing out on the Eternal Vision, which sounded like a long and beautiful sunset. I thought of me and my father passing through Limbo on the way to reincarnation. It didn't make sense that Hindus would stay in Limbo when we had our own business to attend to. I decided we stopped by just to be polite.

I went back to Mabel. Climbed her steady, reaching branches. Sat in her cathedral of crooks and bare twigs. The cold found a slot between my jacket and scarf, invaded the warm cave of air under my sweater. I thought of Limbo. The unbaptized, mingling. Dogs, cats, camels, elephants, tigers, mice, cockroaches, furniture, worms, viruses, Hindus, Muslims, Jews, Jains, Taoists. It sounded like a big party to me.

I remember months later, kneeling on my bed, my elbows on the windowsill, looking out at the rain falling, a sheer, straight thing on the world. On the grass, trees, bees. The air brimmed with the fresh scent of growth. Spring, warm and vocal. Life replenished, thriving. I heard the muted strike of rain on the new leaves of honeysuckle and slender blades of grass. I watched the dogwood trunks darken with wetness.

I stuck my hand out the window. Held it straight, palm facing earth. The rain beaded and rolled off my skin, then dropped to the grass, green and plush, with spots of yellow dandelion and clumps of deep clover. I hoisted myself onto my windowsill, summoning old gymnastic skills, and balanced on my stomach, my body held in a gently rocking fulcrum. The rain fell over my head and back. It wet my hair, slid down my neck. It was good. It was enough.

—〜〜—

Decide for yourself, they said. My mother gave me her library card, worn to the nap of velvet. My father gave me a sheet of graph paper lined with small blue squares. My grandfather gave me the magnifying glass he used for fine print and drove me to the library in his clanking Buick. We coasted over potholes, barely bouncing on the bench seat sprouting maroon stuffing and coiled springs. We circled the library lot, looking for a shade tree, my grandfather leaning forward as he pushed the column on the steering wheel into park, "Go on, dearest. I'll wait."

I took out books. A children's Torah, heavy as a stone. A Koran, river-blue. The graphic Mahabharata in Amar Chitra Katha form—two frugal staples per comic spine. The New Catholic Bible, martyr-red, in a sleeve of thick plastic.

Behind our house was a gap between two wooden slats of fence that I could squeeze through if I turned sideways and blew out all the air in my lungs. I slipped my hand through the gap first, dropped a library book to the ground on the other side, then pushed myself through the slats into the row of yew trees facing the mall parking lot that was littered with broken beer bottles and empty grocery carts careening, unmanned, on windy days. I sat beneath the yew trees, planted a hundred years ago by a farmer that my mother said must have been Irish. A Druid tree, a graveyard tree. I sat there and read to the rustle of hamburger wrappers. The tink of rolling cans. Mosquitoes took my blood for survival. Pavement mica winked, flashed. Heat rose from the parking lot and mixed with shade, the pulse and scratch of summer crickets. I kept my thumbs firm against the margins of each book, my right index finger snaking down quick to turn pages.

It was my favorite place to read holy books. Ants scuttled over Job's pussing boils and Amar Chitra heroines, each face frozen in exact, undiluted emotion: rage, shame, kindness. The vivid comic pages bled turquoise, chartreuse, into my fingers, sweaty with suspense and devotion. Spiders lifted one spindly leg at a time over Lazarus rising. Green yew needles drifted down on Fatima and Guru Nanak. Ogun, Erzulie, Crow, Angulimala. Sacrifice, duty, honor, conviction. My heart broken like an egg tapped against the side of a mixing bowl. Pages smudged where I wept over stories, as real to me as the scars on my knees. Each book suited me. Each book nestled in my palms, leaned against my thighs, with the same good fit.

· I learned from characters and plot, from consequence. The strength of sentences coming together like a fist. I found, among the holy books, strange patterns and commonalities. Strapping St. Christopher ferrying Christ across an unnamed river. Strapping Vasudeva carrying baby Krishna through the waters of the Yamuna. Temptress women. Brotherly betrayals. Cruel acts of kings. Goodness of shepherds. Bread, wine, water, fire. Do unto others. Honor thy father and mother. I ran my eyes over Allah, Lord, Ram, Yahwe, squinting in the glare of sun on white pages. In the Bible, Koran, Torah, creation began with light. In the Mahabharata, creation began with sound. The universe born in a single syllable. The universe born in a single shaft of light. A similarity of narrative opening.

What the holy books had in common, above all else, was story.

—๓—

My first love was Ganesh. He came to me, half elephant, half boy, inter-species, bicultural, in the lilting voice of my father, cross-legged on a fluo-rescent green shag carpet in Smithtown, New York.

Ganesh proved the dignity and importance of secretarial work. He took dictation for Vyasa, and thereby ensured proper transcription of the Mahabharat. As the agreement went, Ganesh would transcribe the epic as long as Vyasa recited the poem continuously.

In the storm of words and writing, Ganesh's pen broke. Still, keeping to the agreement, Vyasa narrated on. Ganesh instantly broke off one of his tusks and used it as a pen. He kept writing and kept his word; he let no bit of story go untended. His body, forever marked by a kept promise. Marked by his devotion to story. His broken tusk repeated eternally in every statue: plastic, gold, wood, mud.

My father was raised in the old Amil Sindhi way of Hindu, Sikh, Sufi, Buddhist. No caste system, a belief in work, simplicity, service, educa-tion. He, my aunt, and grandmother worshipped at the Sufi dargah on Thursdays, the same day they held a *puja* for Veeral Bhagwan. They wore Sikh *kada*, sang the Mool Mantra, fasted for Hindu Shivji and Durgama, quoted the Buddha, rang bells for the Virgin Mary.

No Hindu temples in Vermont; Connecticut; London, Ontario; Smithtown. My father fashioned *aarthi* spaces out of closets, cabinets, small wooden boxes. Lift the lid, a tiny, private *darshan*. The motion of *darshan* need not be large. God is in the details.

Before I went to bed, my father would tell me a Nasruddin story. He pursed his lips with pleasure, the way he did when eating yoghurt. His voice lowered, softened. The same stories over and over again, until I had memorized them and could counter him, tale for tale. In the first telling of his stories, I was a tourist. In every telling thereafter, the story was home. We extracted nutrition from Nasruddin. He made us laugh and think. The Mullah's role always changed—sometimes he played the fool, sometimes he showed up others' foolishness. He hung around with peasants and was rarely found in mosques. His knowledge seemed to come from instinct, and he was always trying to make a decent wage. Sometimes honestly, sometimes not, like the decade he crossed the border from Syria into Libya, once a week, as a smuggler. Every time the border police searched the baskets on his donkeys' backs, they found nothing. Years later, Nasruddin ran into one of the border police, now retired. The man said, "Please, Nasruddin, it drove us crazy trying to figure out what you were up to. All those years, you looked a little richer each time we saw you and your big train of donkeys with empty baskets. Tell me, please, what were you smuggling?" Nasruddin smiled, "Donkeys," he said, "I was smuggling donkeys."

Sometimes my father sat at the edge of my bed and told me stories about Krishna in New York. He said Krishna had come to America in the early 1970s with his flute and tiny suitcase. I suspected they had been on the same flight. In my father's stories, Krishna walked to the mailbox in the middle of a Vermont snowstorm, the tip of his peacock feather showing above the drifts so his cows could follow him. He wrestled a giant snake in the Hudson River under the steady gaze of the Statue of Liberty. He held a flute and dumaroo concert in the subway and left out a tiffin to collect change then donated all the money to St. Vincent's. He bought his curd at Pathmark. He and the gopis rode a school bus through

81

Queens, dancing and singing in the narrow aisle, *pani puri* and *dahi vada* appearing in *Knight Rider* lunchboxes.

Once my mother overheard him. "Ashok," she said, half joking, half serious, "Putting Lord Krishna in a Pathmark. That's sacrilege." He looked at her a moment, then said, "Pears are not found only in Samarkand."

They laughed.

Every night, my mother fell asleep in a pink nightgown with her rosary threaded through the fingers of her right hand. Framed pictures of St. Teresa of Avila, of Little Flower, on her desk. The Virgin Mary on her nightstand. Mother Teresa on the bookcase. A Sacred Heart, flaming, in the bathroom. St. Francis of Assisi on the fridge, holding up the coupons. St. Jude on a laminated bookmark. St. Christopher tucked under the passenger side visor, next to her sunglasses and parking permits. The old Irish way. Throw out the Bible. Keep the saints. In County Kerry, the Sullivans could not read or write or afford a book. But there was always the word, spoken.

I remember my mother saying she was angry with the Vatican for removing St. Christopher's feast day from the universal calendar of saints. "Lack of historical evidence," she spat. "Bloody Pope. The nerve. Who does he think he is, Jesus Christ? Says there's no proof St. Christopher existed. No proof he lived a life of holiness. What in the hell does he have against St. Christopher? And what does proof have to do with anything? What an asshole."

I asked her when it happened, surprised I hadn't heard about it in the news.

"1969," she said. "Year after my mother died. She would have thrown a righteous fit."

"Ma, that was over fifteen years ago."

She snorted. "What's fifteen years? The Crusades happened hundreds of years ago but the same idiots are still fighting. Besides, the Irish forgive but we never forget. My arthritis is ailing me. Go upstairs and get my reading glasses, girl. Next to the lamp. The old grey mare ain't what she used to be."

She said, on hard days, "I must've done something terrible in my last life," and she meant it, dogmatically speaking. She believed in reincarnation. Not that she had been Henry VIII in her last life. But that she could return as a peony. That her sins stacked up against her and she would pay for them, here on earth, and later. She was always striving for enlightenment. "I've had enough," she'd say. "May this be my last time on this accursed earth."

If I had ever called the Pope an asshole, my mother would have snapped her head up and told me to have some respect. But she, baptized, confirmed, wholly Irish-Catholic, was allowed. She had the privilege of insider. She would have thrown a righteous fit to hear any American speaking ill of Gandhi. But if my father grumbled about him and Partition, she merely looked interested and shrugged.

She called herself a Cafeteria Catholic. When I slid my tray along the metal rails in the school lunchroom, I thought of her, picking and choosing, yes Hail Mary, no Crusades, yes evolution, no Inquisition, yes rosary, incense, and bells, no molestation and overpopulation, yes homosexuality, yes heathen husbands and babies. Yes.

If I was mean, she would say, "Don't be un-Christian." I took Christian, by her definition, to mean kind, unselfish, forgiving, inclusive.

Once after reading about Partition, I told her I didn't believe in God any more because religion caused too many terrible things. She was grading papers, and mumbled, "Thomas, Thomas, thou art Didymus." Then, her face crumpled. She looked up at me, sharp, angry, and asked, "What does God have to do with religion?" It was enough, that sentence. I separated the two permanently in my mind and heart.

—∞—

When I was nine I came down with a fever of 106. My father ground aspirin in his mortar and pestle, mixed it with plain yoghurt, salted and peppered, spooned it into my mouth. When my fever did not break, he dunked me in a bathtub of cold water. I remember him pouring ice cubes

83

in the bathtub; they clicked together and knocked solid, cold, against my burning body. The fever stayed, inched higher. I felt my brain boiling. My father gave me a glass of water to drink. Dark grey particles floated in the water—a scoop of the sacred ash of Shirdi, from Sai Baba's eternal flame. He and my grandmother had gone on a pilgrimage to Shirdi before he came to America. For his safety. I drank, the ash coating my tongue in a thick layer. I swallowed and my fever broke, instantly. I remember the feeling of it lifting away from me, like a blanket.

When my mother did not know what to do about something, she prayed on her question to St. Thérèse the Little Flower. Each time she did so, roses came into her life. White, yellow, red, pink. Someone would hand her a rose on the street. A student brought one in to thank her for extra help. Once, she came out of the grocery store and found a rose tucked under her windshield wiper. The roses appeared, and with them, my mother found her answer. "Thank you, St. Thérèse," she said, kissing the Little Flower's picture in gratitude.

At Christmas, we put up a fake tree. It was my job to arrange the limbs and pile them together according to the colored bits of paint at the ends of corkscrewed metal. Then my grandpa and I twisted the boughs into the wooden pole of trunk. We decorated the tree to Bing Crosby and Mario Lanza and James Galway records, hanging my grandmother's 1930s ornaments next to bells and mirrors from India. I loved having a tree in the house, bringing the outside in.

Every year, my mother hung three plastic wise men in the window of the front door. "The Three Men of the East," she said. "Like your daddy." From Christmas Eve till January Sixth, in the old Irish way, we lit a red candle for the Magi to follow. I pictured the Three Men of the East,

When I was eighteen, my mother took me into the garden and stood me near the Sweet William. She grabbed my shoulders and said in a rush: "You're old enough now that I can you tell you the truth. We're English. Just a little bit."

To learn that you are what you've been taught to despise, in a garden, is strange. I remember looking at the geraniums and wondering if they were geraniums. My mother told me about my great-grandmother, the rogue Englishwoman, her father's mother, a DAR who joined the Ku Klux Klan when they marched through Hicksville, Long Island. Julia, newly moved from Hell's Kitchen to suburbia, sucked on cigarettes and cursed the white sheets from behind her locked door. Through a crack in the curtains, she saw her mother-in-law marching with a sign: NO CATHOLICS.

My grandfather, raised Protestant. He met Julia when he was seventeen. She refused to marry him because he wasn't Catholic. He converted. They married at nineteen. His mother was disgusted.

My mother, too, then: a product of love overcoming difference.

For a while I would only admit to being a little bit English if drunk, and then, in a whisper. I crossed myself after saying it. I saw my little bit of English, hunkered down, scared, near my scoliosised hip. Hiding from the others who jeered at it. There was a war in my body.

When I went to Scotland with my Norweigian-Scotch-Irish-Maybe-Blackfoot-Ukrainain-Jewish-by-step-family husband, we spent four

hours in the Museum of Edinburgh. I read the history of the British, their bloodline: Gaul, French, Celt, Viking, Irish, Scottish, Pict. Mixed, like me.

And in England, in Piccadilly Circus, I stood amongst a throng of people. Every fourth Englishman was a woman of South Asian descent.

British—as my grandmothers, mother, and father had known it—
had changed.

—〰—

Mrs. Thompson began with Pakistani, pronouncing Pak like *pack* and
stan like *Stan*. Atirah Jamali and I raised our hands. Mrs. Thompson
moved on to German (I raised my hand), French (I raised my hand), Irish
(I raised my hand), American Indian—no specific tribe; this was 1985—
(I raised my hand).

She quit naming, glared at me and barked: "Indian. From India." I
raised my hand.

Perhaps she thought my mutiny had ended as I did not raise my
hand for Chinese or Portuguese. But then she said Spanish (up went
my hand), then African—no specific country (my hand went up), then
Middle Eastern—no specific country (up went my hand), then Greek.

Mrs. Thompson strode to my desk and pushed down my arm, aloft
for Greek. "Stop raising your hand," she said. "You're making a mockery
of the American diversity lesson."

She said she would call my mother.

I had raised my hand for the members of my family. For my mother,
my father. My ancestors. The immense displeasure of Mrs. Thompson
was disorienting.

She went through religions next. I focused on the world map unrolled
behind her, on the tangerine hip of Brazil, the fuchsia volcanoes of Japan.
I was not accustomed to being upbraided in school so I did not raise my
hand for any religion, but under my desk, I tapped my fingers together for
Hindu, Muslim, Catholic (Mrs. Thompson listed Catholic as different from
Christian). There were others I would have tapped for but Mrs. Thompson
did not name them.

That day, I left school shuffling under the tight nervousness of false
accusation. I was not American if, to be so, there was a limit to the number
of identities one could raise the hand for. It seemed the only explanation.

In me, the sum of my parents' parts became admonished. Absurd. Extravagant.

That night I studied my parents carefully for signs of madness. Although they considered themselves American, maybe no one else did. It seemed a dangerous position. For them and for me.

—⁓—

When I was hurt by other people and their ignorance, my mother said: "Toughen up. Life is suffering. Don't be an emotional cripple. Do you want to be a mindless zombie following the rest? Go your own way. We're born alone and we die alone. Why pretend in-between?" When I said that other mothers let their daughters go to the mall and watch TV and listen to Madonna she'd say, "I don't care what other mothers do. This is what I do and I'm your mother. Period. End of report."

She didn't have time to be wounded by small things. She kept right on going, her own way. So did my father. The only concession they would make to other people and their ignorance was a kind of family wall of silence. We kept to ourselves, for the most part. Sometimes, we'd be cooking or cleaning and my mother would stop what she was doing and look me in the eye and say: "Don't tell anyone our business. Being alone isn't easy but it makes you strong." My father agreed with her. His closest friend was my mother's best friend, Stephan, who had escaped from Auschwitz as a teenager. Stephan never told anyone how he had gotten out and he never talked about his past. He and my father seemed to understand each other; they sat in a companionable silence for hours on end.

Once, in 1986, in North Carolina, near the Haw River, my parents and I went into a store to buy a t-shirt for my grandfather who was not with us. The man behind the counter looked from my mother to my father to me and then back to my mother. He said, "You a Christian, lady?" My mother said yes. He looked at me and pointed and said, "That's disgusting." He reached behind his counter and took out a shotgun. We left his place of business.

91

Once, we were looking for a house in Patchogue, Long Island. The real estate agent stared at my father and said in a voice like a slamming door, "We usually only sell to white couples." My mother's eyes glinted with fight: "That's red-lining; that's illegal. If we report you, your license will be revoked; you could be sent to jail." All day, the man drove us from one end of Suffolk County to the other, my father in the passenger seat, looking out the window, me in the backseat with my mother who leaned forward between the two front seats and kept up a steady stream of civil rights statistics. We saw sixteen houses in one day, houses we could not afford, houses we would never buy. After each house, my mother said, "How about another one?"

—⁂—

My father told me that when a gamma ray burst, gasses poured into space, releasing iron, carbon, oxygen. The iron in our blood, the blood of fleas and zebras—from supernovas. This seemed an even greater journey than Bombay to Kennedy Airport. From stars to our veins. He told me the sound of an exploding star is audible, roughly the F above middle C. For a long time, I would play the F above middle C on my grandmother's piano, over and over, in wonder at the clear tone of stars, my pulse running hot in my green veins. The veins beneath mine and my father's brown arms looked green. The veins beneath my mother's and grandfather's white arms looked blue. Our blood, with the same chromosomes, our veins with the same function. Color as small a difference as two carrots in the crisper. I laid my index finger on that F key, pressed down, felt its sticky release, over and over, until my mother banged pots together and screamed from the kitchen, "For God's sake, play something else. I've got a pack of troubles in here and you're getting on my last nerve."

My father drove the Long Island Expressway, to and from work, playing the Mool Mantra, the sung Sikh prayer, in his tape deck, beating out the rhythm, lightly, against his own chest. He played it loud, like a teenager with Top 40. The words flowed around us. I loved the Mool Mantra, the ache of reach in the singer's voice. At night, I often went with my father on rounds and we listened to the Mantra in the car. He drove fast, singing a line, then popped out the tape so I could repeat it. He told me to focus on the words. He didn't translate. He said just listen to the words, the words themselves. Feel them. It doesn't matter if you understand or not.

He said it the way my mother said to listen to the words of Edna St. Vincent Millay, Walt Whitman. It was a seeking after words. Rhythmic bodies twisting across the page, across my eyes and ears. It was a taking of words into the body, like Communion, like *prashad*. A seeking after words, a seeking after God. A God of paper, a God of trees. A God of ink.

If I missed the school bus, my father drove me. When we passed the first yellow crossing sign, a woman with a purse and a child, I pushed back against the softness of the seat. I dreaded the moment of release, in front of school, all those people milling. Catholics and Christians and Jews. The car door opening, me stepping outside, the Mool Mantra blasting out with me, unknown, alien, to them. I was strangled with the same kind of fear as when my mother said, "Don't put metal in the microwave or it will explode." I eyed the aluminum handles of Chinese take-out boxes with suspicion. So easy to forget, to drop one's guard. I would remain vigilant. I would slip out fast and slam the door quickly to protect the Mool Mantra, my daddy, myself.

Once, some girls standing on the sidewalk looked at me when I stepped from the car then warbled to each other in a made-up language. They did that every time they saw me in the hallways for years afterward. To them, the Mool Mantra simply sounded foreign. Not music. Not holy. Shame ran like a pitchfork through me. The shame of difference. Unprotected, away from the pack. The girls stood close together, filled with the strength of simple corroboration. I've felt that, too. I've known that, too. I've sung that, too. You haven't. You're different.

—⚌—

1986. Calcutta. My cousins and father wanted to rest after lunch but my mother wanted to go outside and see the Dussera festivities, the triumph of good over evil. She brought me over to the neighborhood children, dragging me along while I tried to eat an apricot with one hand. The children shrank from her white skin. White like the Ravana effigy they built. They stared at me, uncomprehending.

The children used gathered sticks and scraps of wire to build Ravana's skeleton. A girl with an orange ribbon at the end of her braid handed me a fizzling *phataka*. She looked like me, with darker hair. I lifted the *phataka* above my head and spun in a circle.

We took pieces of white cloth and paper and soaked them in a flour-water mixture, pasty and adhesive. We covered Ravana's frame with the sticky strips, bestowed him with a triangular nose, bulging eyes, ten arms and nine small heads radiating out in a straight line from his principle head, all with the same expression and features. The children, they let me do the second-to-last Ravana head on the left by myself.

I painted his lips red and attached his hair, gathered from their mothers', sisters', and their own combs, and stuffed into a sack. I wanted my Ravana head to have mine and my mother's hair, reddish-brown. I took the pit of my apricot from my pocket and poked it through a small hole in my Ravana's skull, a brain, so he would not be hollow like the other heads, so he would be different. Looking over at my mother, I saw her standing apart from the shining group of saried mothers, her white arms crossed over her stomach, her shameless legs bare in shorts. I smiled at her and she waggled her fingers at me.

We piled the remaining pieces of wood, wire, paper, and cloth in a circle around Ravana. It felt good to be a We. The girl with the orange ribbon gave me a stick wrapped in a green cloth that reeked of gasoline. Her mother came to us, took matches from a fold in her sari, and told us to stand in a circle around the villain Ravana and be careful with our fire-sticks. She lit her daughter's stick, the girl touched her stick to mine, I touched mine to the child's next to me, and so on, till the circle of us held blazing torches. We held our fires to the heap of tinder around Ravana and the fires merged into one big flame, slowing as it reached Ravana's feet and crept up his body, crackling hot on his main head before sliding across the nine others. When all his heads and arms blazed bright, we stepped back toward the mothers and watched him burn. We saw smoke from other children's fires; boys cheered at the shriek and crash of bottle-rockets. One boy pushed me and yanked on my hair. I whimpered and ran to my mother.

Her eyes dipped into me, a spoon into soup. She said: "What kind of a Sullivan are you? You should have pushed him back. Your great-great-grandmother's rolling in her Kerry grave, right now, as we speak."

I pictured my great-great-grandmother in a patched grey dress, surrounded by rotten potatoes, turning and turning under my feet. It was an odd image to conjure up in a Calcutta back alley. But it made sense to me.

—⚬⚬⚬—

1987. On a fieldtrip to the Hayden Planetarium I sat staring up at a mechanized black dome wheeling with constellations. Virgo, Gemini, Leo, pricks of silver light, connect-the-dot creatures, astrological, glowing. I shared an armrest with Leticia Walker, felt the heat of her fingers. The darkness was thrilling, expectant. Someone could scream. Someone could be kicked or fondled. Someone could weep. The lines of the face, rubbed out in that round, mobile dark. The politics of sixth grade, surrendered.

A woman's voice scratched through the planetarium speakers. "Stars are self-luminous, gaseous bodies made of hydrogen, carbon, oxygen." A few rows back, a boy, most likely Evan Weinstein, shouted "I'm a gaseous body!" and leaned his mouth into the heels of his hands, making the fart noise.

The voice said: "The non-metal elements: hydrogen, carbon, oxygen, are the building blocks of all life." The ceiling shifted in slow, tectonic grace. Time ran over our heads. Plates of stars advanced through the equinox: autumn, winter, spring, summer. I smelled Leticia's perfume, a wilted corsage of pink carnation, sticky hairspray, sliced green melon. I loved the way she harrowed her red fingernails through her bangs. I loved the silhouetted ridgeline of her bra—how it cut her blouse and back in two—a division of maturity I had yet to achieve. Leticia knew, effortlessly, how to be a girl.

Something about the cadence of the voice scratching through the planetarium speakers, something about the words—hydrogen, carbon, oxygen—something about that trinity, brought forth my mother's hand. Her fingers, light as the tread of ants, creating a constellation that linked my forehead, chest, and shoulders.

I remembered standing in her garden, having just watered the zinnias. Their smooth colors and long stems and pretty open faces. Zinnias knew, effortlessly, how to be flowers. There was soil, damp, chilled, in the cracks of my mother's fingers. She leaned her nose into a peony. Eyed a Sweet William with tenderness. Birds sang triplets, *kwee-kwee-kwaa*. I let go of the garden hose. It coiled limp at my feet. The ground rippled with earthworm, beetle, grub. The ground rippled with roots.

On her hands and knees, my mother roamed, snapping off the husked heads of spent flowers. When she got to the zinnias, she said, "In the name of the Father, the Son, and the Holy Ghost." The words sprang from her like a song remembered. I felt the pads of her fingers against me, gentle in press, direct in location. "In the name of the Father, the Son, and the Holy Ghost," she said, again, with a tidy, reflex speed. Her words, in rhythm with touch, made my forehead, chest, and shoulders, hum. Sunlight planked through the swaying trees. My mother's face, cast in a ripe green light. "Blessed are the growing things," she said.

I heard again the small flutter of zinnia leaves. I smelled my mother's hands, fissured from work, filled-in with soil. And in my veins, I felt my blood, ranging with the non-metal elements. In the name of Hydrogen, Carbon, Oxygen. The flesh of star, of zinnia, of Leticia Walker and Evan

Weinstein. In the name of Hydrogen, Carbon, Oxygen. A holy trinity. Fern, woman, mountain, water, pachysandra, snake. It was a matter of combination. A shifted twist of DNA. In the name of Hydrogen, Carbon, Oxygen. *Ek onkar satnaam* Amen *kwa-kwee-kwee*.

—m—

Another memory of my mother in a salwar kameez: powder blue with navy flowers and vines embroidered along the sleeves and neckline. She had the outfit made by a tailor-friend of my aunt's. She ordered a second suit, for me, exactly the same. We had matching blue chunnis, too. My mother loved matching outfits. People thought we were related, more often, when we wore matching outfits.

When the suits first came, my mother thought hers didn't fit right. "I can't move; it's too tight on the sides." I took her cuticle scissors, snipped through the closed seams along the side of the kameez, and slit open the sewn-shut pockets. "How did you know to do that?" she asked me, amazed. I shrugged.

I was good at threading laces through the enormous, accommodating waistbands of salwars. I did it quick, with a safety pin, as my aunt had showed me. My mother always had me close the eyehooks on her kameezes, too, latching them neatly through tiny loops of thread. "I wish they'd put buttons on there," she'd say. "No one but an Indian can get those things closed. You need nimble hands, like yours and your father's."

I remember her, in that blue salwar kameez, drinking tea outside on the patio in Brookhaven. She dipped a spoon into the sugar bowl, drew it out heaping, held it poised above the open steaming circle of teacup then turned the spoon upside down with a decisive flick of wrist. The sugar rained white, battering the surface of the tea, then, disappeared.

"Bloody sugar," my mother said, stirring. Slide of metal on porcelain. "Bloody tea," she said, raising the cup to her lips, sipping between the two words. Her pinkie strayed from the handle of the cup, briefly, something she did to mock fine manners, but then it stuck, and she did it, always, unconsciously.

"Bloody cotton," she said, swallowing, grabbing a fistful of kameez.

My mother saw everything through the prism of history and culture. Her pledge of allegiance to story. To her, all people were historically joined. A shred of plaid from Irish sheep, 1700 BC, unearthed in China. A Mesopotamian seal unearthed in Russia. These bits of evidence, civilizations assumed to be apart but proved connected. "People have never been separate," she said, "People want things, information, each other; they trade, come together."

My mother gave a history lesson with each churn of spoon. She told me how sugar was first grown in India in 550 BC. From India, it went to China, Persia, Egypt, and, in the twelfth century, Crusaders returning from Damascus brought news of sugar to Europe. My mother said soldiers always remember the food and women of the country where they fought and killed and lost loved ones. "And they always bring something home. Even in war, there is exchange." Her eyes took on a subversive glitter.

For five centuries, in Europe, sugar cost one hundred gold pieces per pound. Rich women displayed it in glass jars on their dressing room tables. In 1530, Portugal's King John I ordered life-sized statues of the Pope and twelve cardinals crafted out of sugar. "Imagine slicing the Pope's ear from his head and dropping it casually into a cup of tea from China." I thought of maids coming to dust the tall, silent figures, and when no one was looking, licking their necks.

In the seventeenth and eighteenth centuries the demand for sugar increased along with the demand for coffee and tea. Sugarcane was introduced in South America and the West Indies. The Dutch, English, and French waged war for control. Natives died, whole populations.

1450–1870: eleven million Africans captured and sold into slavery.

Per ton of sugar, one slave died.

My mother quoted: "There is not a barrel of sugar that comes to Europe that is not stained with blood." She said, "I can't remember where I read that line but I've never forgotten it."

Her fingers twitched at her pretty blue kameez. She tapped her foot angrily against the patio of macadam slabs. Weeds grew in the spaces between the slabs. She put me to work weeding the gaps, once a week. She handed me a trowel and said, "Heaven helps a working girl." She hated the untidiness of weeds. I liked weeds and the way nature denies borders by filling them in. Weeds make borders into landscapes, full of life and growth. I felt sad pulling them; they didn't seem lesser than flowers. Just different.

I remember standing next to my mother in Connaught Place, New Delhi. People walking by, staring at her. She didn't notice because she was gazing at a host of marigolds planted in the middle of the road. Plump and luscious orange. She looked stricken, then said, in a voice of mourning, "Mine grow too leggy." Then, reassessing the structure of the plant in relation to human form. "Necky." She touched her own neck.

In every house we lived in, my mother planted marigolds. At the Brookhaven house, she put the marigolds in wooden tubs she had rescued from someone's trash. She nailed the broken slats, sandpapered the rust, gave everything a good coat of paint, and filled the tubs with marigolds. For my father's homesickness. For India.

—⁓—

The day after she announced to the class that if she could exhume Keats she would simultaneously commit adultery and bigamy—to say nothing of necrophilia—by marrying his corpse, my Romantic poetry professor, who reminds me of my mother, who had recently met my mother, and whose children look like clones of the childhood photographs of their mother, said to me:

99

"It must be hard for your mother."

"Yes," I said automatically. Then, "What must be?"

"Having a child who looks nothing like her."

"Yes," I said automatically. One of my hands went to my jaw, the other to my neck.

—∞—

When we are alone together, my mother curses excessively. She is a woman who, as she says, "Rises to the occasion," and, "Takes responsibility for her actions."

With these phrases, she condemns and implicates anonymous (and familiar) people who do *not* rise to the occasion, who do *not* take responsibility for their actions. All of my mother's aphorisms must be inverted in order to be fully understood.

My mother is a teacher, an educator. She will not curse in front of *her* children; she will not be a bad example. But when she is alone, in front of her real child, her only child (as I jealously remind her), she curses with grit and proficiency. It makes me feel special, more myself. It makes her feel unfettered, more herself.

Her two favorites:

"Fuck a snake at midnight."

"Shit on a ten-foot rock."

I love the specificity of both.

"Ma!" I say. "Your language!"

"I'm Irish," she snaps, as if I wouldn't understand, as if I am not Irish, too, although a lesser percentage than her. It is like that for children. We are all a lesser percentage of our parents.

—∞—

"Dr. Bunoup," my mother says. "Now there was a man with a mind." She refers to the curator at the Cairo Museum whom we met and befriended in 1988. When I was six, my mother brought me to see the mummies at the Metropolitan Museum in New York. She taught me to read hiero-glyphics; she taught me that there is a beginning and an end to every-thing; she taught me that death could be gold-leafed and opulent if you had the money to pay for such things. We lapped up books about Queen Hatshepsut, ruler of Egypt for twenty-one years. We marveled at the Queen's decadence, her imagination—Hatshepsut, who purchased a forest from the coastal East African kingdom of Punt. On a school of ships, the trees were sailed to her, then planted around her palace; she hired armies of men to hydrate the trees: five, six, seven times a day. A woman who attached a king's beard to her chin; a woman who kept alive a forest in the middle of a desert. She fascinated us both.

My mother followed up on our New York learning by taking me to the source. When I was eight, we went to Egypt with my father on a doctor swap mission. We saw more mummies. We saw more granite statues and learned that, in the frontal pose, those with clenched fists were men, and those with relaxed hands, female. We liked Akhenaton, the mad fanatic.

"Why was Dr. Bunoup a man with a mind?" I ask. I have heard this story hundreds of times.

"When he first met us, he pointed to you and said to me, 'She has your facial bone structure—square jaw—and your long neck.' Now this is a man who knows faces, painted on sarcophagi or not; he knows bones dating from 2180 BC. This is a man who studies things like faces and bones. If he sees this in us, it must be true."

"It must be," I say.

I remember feeling embalmed, a specimen, when he indicated to his assistant what a mandible at a ninety-degree angle looked like. He used a thin, wooden pointer. He touched it to my mother's jaw, and then to my own.

—∞—

"Your father," she says and then says nothing more. We stand accused, my father and I. Her tone is a wrecking-ball. We are crushed.

101

"Your father was not in the room when you were born. He was off taking care of some diabetic lacking in self-control (like your grandfather) who had eaten too much cake. He always said medicine was his first love. Get a good job. With benefits. Never rely on a man. The nurse took you away to be cleaned (he looked just like the man Cousin John dated before he met Jim), and while you were gone, in waltzes your father. He says, 'Hiya!' Just like that, 'Hiya!' I could have strangled the son-of-a-bitch. Then the nurse comes back into the room with you, but he's already forgotten who your mother is. The woman next to me was sleeping. The nurse looked at her then looked away. He looked at me and looked away. He looked at your father and then down at you and then that excuse for a nurse hands you to your father. You were mine. I had carried you in my womb for nine months. It was my right to be handed you. I earned it. So what if you looked like your father?"

—m—

At the end of every long day, my father came home and took off his glasses and washed his face. Sometimes at eleven, sometimes at one or two in the morning. I waited up for him and perched on the bathroom counter while he soaped and rinsed. When he had toweled his face dry, we played a game in the mirror. We looked at ourselves. We argued. You look like me; no you look like me; no you look like me; those are my eyes, that is my chin, that is my nose. No, it's mine. But I came first, he would say. We would laugh.

I remember once, passing a mirror, catching sight of myself, when we lived in Vermont. It was summer. I was darker than my father. I stopped and felt an instant of shock. I was different from my mother. I was different from everyone around me at school, in the supermarket, in half of my family. It was a strange moment—the realization of surface difference.

Why this preoccupation with ratios? With percentages? With drops of blood? What is it about human beings and purity? Dilution? Do people see mixing as a form of erasure, bit by bit? But what if it is an act of recovery? What if it is an act of survival? What if we are saving you? What if without the half-breeds you would already be gone? We are marked with our in-betweenness. On our in-between bones, hair, skin, minds, souls.

—◊—

In Arizona, at the Grand Canyon, I saw my first mule. My father explained, "It's a cross between a horse and a donkey. They're sterile." I was fourteen.

Standing between my parents, later that day, I overheard a ranger calling me a mulatto.

Suddenly, I understood the root of the word. Suddenly, I loved mules.

The first time I went to a doctor for adults, my mother came with me. The doctor told her I might have trouble getting pregnant (I was seventeen) because my hips were so narrow.

This made sense to me. After all, I was a mule. But my mother was livid. She called the doctor a White Devil, an Ignoramus. I barely had time to dress before she pulled me from his office.

When we got home, she photocopied her Asian geography test map: all purple borders and amorphous shapes—no names. She wrote in: China, India, Pakistan, Bangladesh, Thailand, Indonesia, Sri Lanka, Vietnam. She wrote the population for each country beneath its name. At the very top of the page she wrote NARROW-HIPPED PEOPLE OF THE WORLD and mailed it, express, to the doctor.

—◊—

Why do people think I don't look like my mother? If you listen to me, I look like her. If you tell us a joke, we will laugh at the same line. If you look at me quickly, in left profile, you will see her in my face.

Inside me, half an Irishwoman. Reckless and wailing in red boxing gloves. She is maudlin; she is extravagant. She is invisible.

There was always a moment of surprise, in the seventies and eighties, and the first half of the nineties, when seeing another Indian. We were rare. Later, my father would say, "We're taking over," because there were so many South Asians, everywhere, anywhere. But when I was a child and teenager, it was unusual. You got used to being the only one, to feeling like the only one. When we happened to see other Indians we threw quiet secret glances, like spies. To Americans, Indian was Indian. To Indians, Indian meant: what kind? Punjabi, Gujarati, Malayali? Muslim, Hindu, Jewish, Christian, Sikh? What kind? *Kahan say?* From where?

When my grandmother lived with us in Vermont, she and my father would sometimes fight in Sindhi. There was no need to shut a door or stand in the backyard or go in another room. They simply switched languages and argued in that privacy. My mother would look at me and say, "She's winning; now, she's got him." I would ask how she knew. She would say, "I may not understand the words, but I know exactly what's being said. Just listen. That's the sound of a mother winning."

Why does being yourself have to be confusing? An acquaintance, Indian, vegetarian, once asked me about my mother and how she practiced Hinduism. I said, "In an Irish-Catholic kind of way." He laughed and said, "She's Sindhi, right? Or is she Punjabi?" I said, "She's Irish-Catholic." His chin dropped low on his neck. He was shocked. He had always assumed I was "Just Indian." He said, "But when did this happen?" I laughed, "When I was born." He asked, "But how did you eat dinner together?" The question surprised me, as did his worry. I said, "My mother and grandfather ate meat, my father and I didn't. My mother always used a different spoon to stir each pot. We all pitched in and cooked different meals or sometimes everyone ate vegetarian, like when we had pasta." My friend looked exhausted from what he considered the effort of it all. To him, the borders crossed at the dinner table, the compromises and sacrifices were too much.

My mother was punctual. My father, loose. Indian Standard Time, she would howl, accusingly. He'd try to hurry, and wasn't often late, but he was nowhere near the terrifying punctuality of my mother. His insides didn't tick to the same clock. If I complained about mowing the lawn, my father would say, "Okay, do it later." If I said I would do better in math class, he'd ask me how sure I was, "Fifty percent, eighty percent, one hundred percent?" He thought in degrees. She thought in binaries—right, wrong, yes, no. If I complained about making my bed, she said, "I wish I had a mother. One day I'll be dead and you'll regret this moment. Sharper than a serpent's tooth, a thankless child." She had a way of stripping things down to what was most elemental with one flash from her grey-blue eyes. She'd say, "The truth hurts, Neela Ashok. Tell the truth and shame the devil." Or, "Your word is your bond." Words, the embodiment of self, not to be squandered, violated, cheapened. When she wanted my most solemn promise, she stuck out her pinkie and said, "Give me your word, on your mother's soul."

My father had a tenderness for food. He would pick up a tomato, holding it in his hand and address it, "*Arrey, bhai, kaisa hai?*" Brother, how are you? He considered the body of each vegetable, the shape of it, and cut accordingly. He didn't eat meat but he carved it for my mother and grandfather. He looked at a chicken and knew where its bones and organs lay and sliced accordingly, with grace and precision.

My mother had a practical approach to food. She liked dark meat, grizzle, scraps, leftovers. Her parents' room had smelled of ripe bananas because my grandfather hid them under the bed, out of habit; as a boy, he had saved his delivery money to buy bananas, only to have his brother steal and eat them. My grandmother also stored food under the bed. Cans of peas, soup, Spam, corn, stewed tomatoes. Both had a fear of starvation. One, raised on Flatbush Avenue. One in Hell's Kitchen. Both went through the Depression. My mother ate quickly, having been raised around a big hungry family, everyone reaching and racing for food. Her approach to food was: "Eat it, excrete it." It needed to be ingested for utilitarian purposes, to keep working, to keep going. Waste not, want not.

My father savored his bites. He nodded in appreciation after every swallow. He put a good ratio of pea to potato on each forkful. "Take rest," he'd say. "Take it easy. Good for digestion."

On August 15th, my mother celebrated the Feast of the Assumption, the Blessed Virgin's reception into heaven. On August 15th, my father noted Indian Independence Day, but did not celebrate. "No British," he'd say. Then, "No Sindh." A hole of refugee silence.

Facing a sunset, he waxed poetic about light refraction, cloud density, spectral colors. His appreciation was for mechanics: how the sunset came to be was beautiful to him. My mother would listen up to a point, then put her hands over her ears and say, "I don't care how it got here. It's enough for me that it's beautiful." He had the same reaction to her sociopolitical explanations. He'd sip tea as she expounded on hegemony, then twist his hand noncommittally and say, "What you say is true. But tea tastes good. So I will have more."

She said, "I love you," easily, especially when getting off the phone. He showed it but never said it, unless writing it in a birthday card. She was always turning down the heat to save money. He was always turning it up to warm his desert bones. She reused tea bags and paper towels, a recycler, threatening us with the extinction of the rain forest in the 1970s well before it was fashionable. She planted chicken carcasses in the garden to enrich the soil. He found all of that unsanitary. He used three different sponges when cleaning: one for the counter, one for the sink, and one for the dishes.

They both believed in the mask of dignity. Even if you don't feel proud and strong, put your chin up. Never let them see you cry. Lessons in how to handle being strange. She had been born strange, passionate, and wild, which is its own burden. When she was angry, she screamed and grabbed and flung things: tissue boxes, pans, across the room. She banged doors, made herself seen and heard. When she was sad, she wailed and hollered and pounded her fists on the floor. When she was happy she laughed loud and long and rocked her body back and forth. My father was strange, wild, and passionate, too, but he did not express these things physically or as loudly as my mother. They both understood how such things as strangeness, passion, and wildness cannot be kept down in a person; it must be expressed. It was what they had in common, a sense of faith, passion, work, service, immigrant drive, and a reverential belief in education. They may have been from different cultures, but their value systems, the way they thought and saw the world, at root, were the same.

Sameness doesn't make something whole. Difference doesn't make something incomplete. There is always the other. Sometimes outside yourself. Sometimes inside. My home, my family, seemed perfectly normal and mundane to me, no matter how much other people tried to pin the exotic and rare onto us.

—m—

My mother read *A Passage to India* when she was sixteen and we watched it as a family, on PBS, in 1989. I was fifteen years old. My grandfather sat on the couch and my parents and I sat on the floor with our backs against the couch. The ghosts of the British hanging in the air, my mother muttering, "Divide and conquer," savagely, at the screen. She saw Divide and Conquer in everything, in the machinations of every world government and religion, in the teacher's union, in the packs of popular teenagers roaming the hallways of her school. "If people would just stick together and rise up. It's all about Divide and Conquer." We were all quiet during the scene when Adela disappears into the caves of Ajanta and Ellora. "Oh no, oh no, I can't watch, I can't bear it," my mother said and covered her face with her little hands. She was the only one of us who had read the book, so she knew what was about to happen. My father was silent. They sent me out of the room during the "rape" scene. They said, simultaneously, "Go make tea," as they always did whenever sex or violence came on the TV. I remember

107

standing outside the closed door, hearing a woman scream. I remember my mother saying, "That poor, poor man. Destroyed by a hysterical white woman."

I made four teas and brought them in on a tray. My father plucked at some crumbs in the carpet. He looked at my mother and said, "We should vacuum the floor in here." My mother, who did most of the cleaning, snapped, "What's this 'We,' White Man?" There was a pause. Then we all laughed and laughed.

—ʍ—

Working on model trains, HO gauge, was what my father and I did to relax on weekends. We went down into the dank cobwebbed basement, filled with soggy boxes, and alternated, from his head to mine, the blue-and-white engineer cap my mother had bought us. Whoever wore the hat got to work the controls. We set his pager near the speedometer so we would hear it when it went off.

My father loved German model train stations. We spent months gluing and painting them. It was something he started doing before I was born, in the intern housing of Glen Cove. The passionate absorption of the miniature, the comfort in creating a universe. We had one main junction with a gabled roof and green shutters. Tiny pine trees dotted the lawn. Red benches flanked the black-and-white signal tower. My father had made the station when I was one year old. He called it Neela Junction and painted my name on the sign next to the clock, forever stuck at 2:53.

We created a world. Half of the basements of each house we lived in were filled with particle boards balanced on sawhorses and little Teutonic villages. Trains blinking merrily, tooting along. The boiler clanking, firing. The floorboards above us creaking with my mother's and grandfather's steps. My father worked four jobs, as a doctor, scientist, nutritionist, and lecturer. He hardly slept and didn't seem to miss it. Sundays with the trains were when we spent time with each other. We sat together in silence, except for the necessary words.

108

Our speedometer was a small bronze box with a black handle that spun in a circle. We knew which engines could go at what speed, depending upon how many cars were attached. My favorite was a little yellow engine, a caboose, really, that flew with a chunky steady beat over the tracks. I named her Runaway. She was dense, strangely heavy, even though she was much smaller than the other engines. She could be taken up to eighty and often went flying off the tracks but somehow survived every crash and fall. My father liked the Santa Fe engine and the Amtrak dining car, a pan-colored silver, black silhouettes of people in the white-papered windows, as if seen by night, with the shades drawn. Smooth, sleek, elegant, reliable.

It was my job to clean the oxidation off the brass and copper alloy tracks. I used an eraser and rubbed the tracks in slow, careful strokes until the rails gleamed gold. Some engines, like Midnight, tipped over unless the tracks shone immaculate. We had a tunnel made of Styrofoam, cut from a test-tube container my father brought home from Brookhaven National Lab. We cut it into a curve and painted it with moss, trees, and rocks and set it over the tracks, north of Neela Junction, before the rise of town. It was thrilling to see the train disappear into the tunnel then roar out the other side. We bent down to watch Midnight's front headlight flickering in the darkness like a third eye. It was thrilling to slow the train at the crossing, lower the black-and-white-striped bar, set the red lights blinking. The tiny wagon pulled by tiny horses, waiting to pass.

Those Sundays in the basement, my father relived his childhood on the railroad tracks. It brought back his father. He passed on to me an approximation of his past, weaving stories of home, of family, with each chug and clank of the model trains.

When his beeper went off, I went with him to the hospital for rounds. He never left work, it was always with him. He saw everything through the prism of science and the body. His pledge of allegiance to story. The way to make him remember a person was to state their disease. "The one with jaundiced skin." "The one who had bad arthritis." "Okay, okay, no problem," he would say. "Now I remember."

Once, he and I went through the drive-through Dairy Barn to get some milk. We made small talk with the clerk who opened the sliding door. When she handed us the milk, my father looked at her hand wrapped around the bottle. He said to her, "Are you thirsty all the time?" She looked taken aback. "Is your hair feeling especially dry lately?" She nodded, stunned. He said, "You should tell your doctor to check your thyroid. It's nothing to worry about, but if you go to the doctor you'll feel better soon." Then he smiled, rolled up the window, and we drove home.

His mother, brother, and sister all died while he lived in the States. He missed their funerals, the distance too long to reach in time. He treated other people's pain, during the funerals, oceans away.

—⚬—

After Vietnam, my uncle Woody heard the dog talking to him in the voice of the devil. Hanging the dog from a tree in the backyard was his first schizophrenic break. He was institutionalized more than ten times, but every time he figured how to fool the doctors and got out, something my mother said with pride and fear. No one seemed to understand my uncle; he was happiest alone, living on the street. He had stayed with my grandfather, mother, and father, in the Hicksville house, from when I was born till I was one and a half, when he tried to strangle me. My mother found him with his hands around my neck and she put him out of the house.

No matter where we moved, my grandfather had a post office box. He said it was because he didn't want me to see his pin-up girl magazines in the mailbox. But it was really so he could get letters from my uncle Woody. My mother forbade him from telling Woody where we lived. Our phone number was always unlisted. But family is family, and my uncle appeared at every house.

110

Once, when I was eight, he came to the house in Nesconset, needing money. My father was at work, my grandfather out with an accounting client, and my mother didn't have any money on her. I had thirty-seven dollars saved from the past two years of helping my grandfather fill out tax returns. While my mother stood in the doorway, hiding me with her little body, trying to tell her brother that she really didn't have any cash in the house, I ran upstairs and got my thirty-seven dollars from under my mattress, where I kept it, like my grandpa told me to. I squeezed past my mother and gave my uncle the money, a little worried he might try to strangle me again. "You don't have to pay me back," I told him. "It's yours." I could smell the wild stench of homelessness on him. He hadn't cut his hair or beard or nails in years. In a way, he didn't seem so different to me than our family. Wandering, living light. Doing his own thing, sticking out. But the look in his eye scared me. He smiled like he had a secret, took the money, and went sloping down the driveway, under the blooming cherry tree, pink petals drifting against the blacktop. My mother shut the door. She was pleased. "Well, you're Irish all right. That was good of you."

When my father came home, she told him the story. "Good Sindhi girl," he said, and patted my head.

They didn't begrudge the other's blood, but each claimed me for their side.

Once in China, on a teacher's tour and doctor swap, after we had been living in hotels for a month or so and drifting to a new town each night, I said to my mother, "Let's go back home and rest." She snapped, "It's a hotel, not a home," tired of wandering, tired. I said, "Any room we're in all together is home to me." Something in her face softened, and her necessary hardness dropped for a moment. "Who's your mother?" she said, with a touch of pride, the words running together, the emphasis dropped from "your."

If I ever made her mad, she would use the same phrase, "Who's *your* mother?" with great disgust. Your behavior said everything about your mother. About how you were raised and where you came from. She sent

111

me off to school every morning, saying, "Learn everything. Be good. Don't shame the family name." She meant Sullivan, she meant Vaswani. She meant both.

—ᴍ—

At night, I'd wait till my parents went to bed then cross the hall to my grandfather's room. I was the only person allowed to open his door without knocking. We stayed awake half the night, watching boxing on the sly. My parents did not permit me to watch television but my grandfather had a little set with bent rabbit ears that he kept on his dresser. His room fell outside house rules. The set fuzzed over, grey static blipping across the middle of the screen. We accepted the fuzz as intrinsic to every show we watched, a common plotline. Because my grandfather was deaf he listened to the TV with a plastic earphone shaped like a flying saucer. It plugged into the TV and stretched about two feet. We'd pull up two chairs, our knees pushed against the knobs of the dresser, so my grandfather could see the TV and the earphone cord could reach his ear. He held the earphone up to his left ear and I sat next to him listening to the tinny echo of voices. He always rooted for The Black or The Irish in every fight. If there wasn't a Black or Irish, he'd root for the underdog, whoever it was. When something happened in a fight that displeased him, he'd start to shout, then remember my sleeping parents, slap his hands against his knees, roll his eyes heavenward, shake his head sadly. During commercials, we either played penny poker or I cut his thick yellow toenails since he had trouble bending over. He'd laugh whenever I moved my hand against his foot, and say, "Tickles," and I'd say, "Hold still, Grampie." We argued over who was more devious, more glamorous, Linda Carter (his choice) or Jackie Collins (mine). We tuned in for *Solid Gold* on the weekends. Those long-legged women in leotards shingled with glitter. Feathered headdresses swaying like large birds. Bawdy Madame jokes. My grandfather loved Madame. For her, he'd throw back his head and laugh his biggest laugh, full of shock and pleasure. If he

112

laughed too hard, he reared back, and the earphone cord unplugged from the TV, canned laughter suddenly blaring through the room. I'd spring forward and lower the volume with a fast twist of the sliver knob so we wouldn't get caught by my parents. He'd lift his white, shaggy eyebrows at me and wink. Sometimes I cleaned out his closet, arranged his fedoras, Panamas, bowlers, galoshes, seersucker suits, dress shirts in varying shades of baby pink, blue, yellow, mint green. My mother and I always admired his ability to wear the softest, most feminine pastels and look like a big strapping man.

All summer, while my parents worked, my grampa and I read Danielle Steele and Agatha Christie and Louis L'Amour side by side on brown plastic kitchen chairs, passing a roll of shiny blue Life Savers back and forth. Sometimes we ate a lunch of orange things. Kraft macaroni and cheese, orange juice, a halved grapefruit that we dug at with ridged spoons we'd bought at the Flea Market. We folded our grapefruit halves into football shapes, squeezed the juice into bowls then slurped it out. At dusk, we wandered into the backyard and he pitched tennis balls to me that I hit with a red plastic bat. We picked trees for first, second, and third base, and I'd run, tapping their trunks with my hand as I went by. I'd pitch balls for my grampa, too, but I had to run the bases for him. He'd holler, "Go go go, run run run," and wave his hands in the air, just like he did for Darryl Strawberry and Gary Carter.

I was always shouting so my grandfather could hear what I said. When my mother came home from work, she'd say, "Pipe down. I'm not deaf, you know."

I never asked him about my grandmother Julia or uncle Woody. When he picked me up, I smelled the pain of those losses on his neck, just behind his ear, masked by Old Spice and a ground-up mineral smell, like Flintstones vitamins.

He didn't have a pension or money saved. Nothing but a little Social Security and some income he made from old loyal clients, the ones still alive. It was a big fun outing to go with my grandpa to see his tax return clients. He'd put on a three-piece suit, a pastel shirt, a hat, and slip his ivory shoehorn into the backs of his freshly shined shoes. His shoes always matched his suit, and his hat, too. Most of all I loved his briefcase with little gold locks that clicked open and shut in tidy efficiency.

He was a man who liked to have a good time. It drove my mother crazy that he ate doughnuts and drank whiskey even as his diabetes worsened. "No discipline," she'd say. "Self-indulgent." But I loved my grandfather's easy-going joy. I wanted to protect his freedom. I snuck him doughnuts and whiskey late at night.

—❧—

My mother always hummed while she ironed my father's work shirts. The smell of the iron steaming, smoothing cuffs stitched by Indian tailors. No American store-bought shirt ever fit my father. They were all too big. My mother hummed high reedy versions of "Silver Dagger," "Molly Malone," "Paddy's Lament," coasting the iron over my father's slender Calcutta sleeves. She sang the few words she remembered, startling, here and there in her humming. When she was truly happy, she sang, "O Sacred Head, Now Wounded," her favorite hymn, a grim and gruesome Lenten dirge. She knew all the words to that one.

American shirts fit me, but pants were always too long and too big in the waist. "Clothes made for giant Americans," my mother grumbled and took out her sewing basket. She folded my pant cuffs under, pinned a quick line. "In your country," she'd say, "people are properly sized. They don't take up too much space." By *your country*, she meant India. She always called India "your country." Or "your and your father's country." In dressing rooms, she drew the curtain then sat on the bench and watched me try on outfit after outfit. "They're all swimming on you," she'd say, and sigh, "Lean hound for the long race. We'll have to take your britches in and up. Christ almighty." I felt sorry for her and the extra work.

Sometimes I imagined her having a child that looked just like her and fit into American clothes. I told her that once and she said, "That's ridiculous. What would I do with a child like that?"

My father taught himself to play guitar by ear, the way all Indian musicians learn music, sitting cross-legged. I always thought "sitting Indian style" meant sitting like a Native American; it didn't occur to me that the way my father and I sat naturally, comfortably, was Indian style. We were always cross-legged on the floor or squatting. Our bodies just went that way. My mother sat next to us in a chair, fondly patting her "arthritic Irish knees."

Both of my parents loved Simon and Garfunkel. My mother had gotten my father into them and he taught himself the chords to "The Boxer," singing it as only an immigrant could, like the words were made for him. He sat, head hung over the guitar, and strummed, sad, soft, sweet-voiced. He never said the words reminded him of himself but he didn't have to. We knew, my mother and I. We sat and listened and cried as he sang. Cried for him, for ourselves, for our family, for the ache of lonely, endless, landless wandering.

When I left my home and my family, I was no more than a boy
In the company of strangers
In the quiet of the railway station, running scared

Mmm, mmm, mmm. . . .

For a long time, whenever I saw a baby, I would cry. I thought of babies as immigrants. Coming from their mothers into a new world. Learning to breathe air. A new language and environment. Babies seemed capable of withstanding great trauma, like birth, but also fragile. They were starting fresh. I would look at my father in wonder. Thinking of how far he had come. He never talked about any of it, never seemed to think much of the distances he had crossed, all he had learned, how he had changed. He worked, thrived in his work, and took care of his family, without complaint.

He and my mother loved New York. They loved the place as a shining beginning, where everyone in my family landed first and stayed longest. They loved it for the way it let people be themselves without worry or shame. New York absorbed my family in a way no other part of the country ever could.

SOMETHING IS ALWAYS LOST

September 12, 2001. I volunteered at Chelsea Piers—FEMA's temporary morgue and animal shelter.

Nearby, hanging huge above the empty, eerie, military-monitored West Side Highway, a billboard for the Hallmark Channel. The words stacked in the form of a skyscraper:

STORY

UPON

STORY

UPON

STORY

UPON

STORY

UPON

STORY

I sat at the missing persons desk—a pockmarked, splintered picnic table—and entered information on forms still warm from a photocopy machine: Name, Hair Color, Eye Color, Age, Identifying Marks, Last Seen Wearing. Everyone I spoke to was missing someone. Every detail given by a mother, lover, brother, friend, daughter, uncle, wife, was told in the form of a story.

On that day, I came to believe in the hope of present tense:

"He has bullet scars here, here, and here—Vietnam. Shot three times in the same hour"; "She was born in Kerala, and has a small pox vaccination scar on her upper right arm"; "He's 6'2" and blonde like

119

his grandma"; "Her hair is in cornrows and she's wearing her wedding band"; "Last year, when he was twenty, he had all his wisdom teeth out at once—drank milkshakes for weeks. Strawberry. He only likes strawberry"; "She is wearing a black dress and a silver Timex on her left wrist and she had her appendix removed when she was nine. It burst while we were riding the log flume at Disneyland"; "He has his mother's eyes. Brown. Bits of green at the center."

One woman brought a comb wound with strands of her daughter's hair. Her hands trembled as she gave me a vial of insulin, "She's diabetic and will need it. It's been twenty-four hours."

I put the insulin and comb in a Ziploc bag. Her daughter, a shoulder-length redhead.

Later that day I went to Ground Zero with a Red Cross shipment of masks and tarps. A line of doctors, nurses, paramedics, stood on the rubble, waiting for someone to be dug up alive. At St. Paul's Church, the gravestones were buried in ash and I handed sandwiches to cops. Wading through the knee-deep scattered paperwork of the World Trade offices, I saw what might have been a finger. The 500 names I had entered on forms scrolled before me in the air. I showed the body part to a fireman with burning, stricken eyes. I was too afraid to pick it up myself.

That night, I lay in bed next to my husband. I cannot speak of this in past tense.

While he sleeps, I memorize the geography of his scars—one above his left eyebrow that cuts into the hair, from when his brother pushed him off a swing. A gash along his left calf from the kickstand of a bike. Three slices in his shoulder—self-inflicted razoring for an avant-garde midnight theater piece. A nick beneath his nose from falling down a flight of stairs. Crescent at the corner of his mouth (right side, close to top lip) from a skinhead with a mohawk who drew blood with a knife. Two tattoos. One on his back left shoulder blade: a family crest, Scottish, his father's and brother's names and the dates of their births and deaths. One around his right ankle: barbed wire representing the fencing of his uncle's cattle ranch in Montana, the miles he has worked there. Slight astigmatism in the right eye. Mole on left temple. Royal toe, both feet. Scar from hernia surgery as a boy. Broken arm from falling out of tree on a camping trip. All toes and fingers broken at least once from football at a Quaker school. Thirteen cavities.

There are invisible scars on my husband's body. When he was a year and a half, a babysitter and her boyfriend put out thirty-six cigarette butts on his arms and legs. The scars healed. His young skin: elastic, indestructible. He has no memory of it.

Some pain can be felt then forgotten. Little wounds that shape us.

—꩜—

The first place I traveled by subway, September 14, 2001, was to the Museum of Natural History. The Middle Eastern Wing: empty. The muezzins sang from the speakers. I stood in front of *Sindh* and saw myself reflected in the glass.

Once every few months, throughout my childhood, my parents and I went to the Museum of Natural History. I would say, "I am going home," and stand in front of the exhibit marked *Sindh* in the Hall of the Asian Peoples. We could not go to Sindh. It had been absorbed into Pakistan. They did not let our kind of Sindhis back into the country. It made my father sad. We stood there together and thumped our fingers against the display glass. We looked at the red tassels of *jutay*, a small pair of shoes. Then, the tassels, bright red. Now faded. Even protected from sunlight, color fades.

The mannequin of Sindh is faceless. Her *chunni* and clothing hang on a wire frame. She is mere structure.

As a child, seeing that slim exhibit made me understand Sindh as something lost, a place of the past for me and my family. Our origins. Our fossil.

When I see an exhibit on India, I want to call my cousins. I want to take a pen and correct the neat, tidy statements hanging next to the

121

artifacts. I want to cross it all out and write the names of my family. Write the places we live, scattered, across the planet.

There is isolation behind that thick transparency. Glass reflects, distorts.

—∾—

My mother has a passion for museums. She fans herself provocatively over Picasso exhibits. Swoons for Yoruban masks. I was eight when she took me to the Museum of Natural History to hear Richard Leakey speak. My mother loves evolution with the subversive delight of a Catholic schoolgirl. She read to me from *The Sex Contract*. We studied Jane Goodall's face.

What I gleaned from Leakey's lecture: We are all African. We are all related, with a common ancestor. We are family.

I also decided Richard Leakey was wrong. If he were me, he would not look for the missing link. *Australopithecus* mated with *A. Afarensis*; *Neanderthal* with *Homo sapiens*. We are their spawn. In the ground, no explanatory skeleton that will form a neat line of progression. What came between hominids: sperm and egg. What came between them was you and me. The mixed being.

I do not believe in missing links. I believe in sex. The bee coated in pollen, seeds in a gale, a log floating a lizard across a river, a human reclined in coach-class.

I believe in portability.

I put a picture of Richard Leakey up on my wall even though I did not fully agree with him.

At the Museum of Natural History, there was a butterfly, I remember, that appeared to be a leaf. At first glance, I thought it was a mistake, a bit of foliage fallen into the case.

When a caterpillar enters the pupal stage, its skin splits; it does not move or feed. Larval tissues dissemble and reorganize. Same cells, same matter, different form. After ten to fifteen days, the chrysalis ruptures. An adult butterfly hauls forth. Transformation. Caterpillar into butterfly. So unlike each other, they require a different name. Do they long for the other name? The name that was lost? The scorched name of the beloved? Caterpillar into butterfly. From earth to air. And inside the pupae, a secret life.

There is always something unremembered, irretrievable, when moving from one identity to another. There is always something lost.

In the womb, bone and flesh develop simultaneously. There is no order, no hierarchy of one above the other.

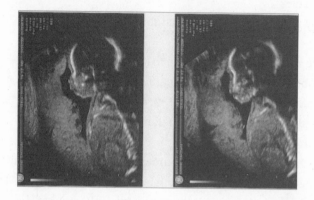

But on the body, there exists a linear hierarchy, from top to bottom. It is possible to lose from the bottom up and live, but not from the top down. There is significantly less terror in the phrase, "Off with her feet." To humans, what is on top is higher, better.

What does it do to a human being to categorize by shape: fat, skinny, tall, short? By bank account? Color? Sexuality? Religion?

The continuation of life depends upon difference—the wider the gene pool, the stronger the spawn. My uncle-in-law, a Montana cattle rancher, calls it hybrid vigor. He keeps the sperm of his bulls in the fridge, next to the Ranch dressing. He bites into a hamburger and speaks of it like family: "This is old 502. She was a good mother and had a nose for finding water. A natural leader." There is a genuine honor in knowing what you eat. In having loved it.

At the Museum of Natural History, a butterfly. It has been tagged. Named:

Western pygmy blue

Brephidium exilis

Captured by Anonymous

3 July 1963

In a lemon grove. Orange County, California.

The body, in death. A black, downy thorax. Two pairs of wings. Mahogany, silver, blue, white. Skewered with pins. Mounted, tagged, above a ruler.

Its wingspan, petite. Three-eighths of an inch.

[   ]

The violence that can be done to three-eighths of an inch.

What is essential to our fascination is what we maim.

For the butterfly, I do not approve of the plushy, idle word: *flutter*. It is only used because of the false equation: small = delicate.

Those wings are throbbing.

Butterflies see in pixels like Seurat and television. They see ultraviolet wavelengths on flowers and the wings of other butterflies. They see polarized light and track in it the precise tilt of the sun.

As the butterfly beats its wings, the shingled scales tip and reflect, iridescent. To a creature who sees ultraviolet, the butterfly flickers, communicates, in flight.

We do not see ultraviolet. We are burned by it.

When my dog Lugnut chases squirrels, he looks up into trees; when he chases rabbits, he hunts among bushes. He ignores geese because he knows he can't fly. He sniffs around garbage bags (only on 16th Street and 8th Avenue, near Rebar) for rats. He knows when I carry the laundry bag where we are headed. He knows when I take out a suitcase that I am leaving. He knows when I change from flip-flops to sneakers that I am going outdoors. He looks at my shoes, then up at me and he knows. He knows which delis have cats and which have biscuits behind the counter and he knows that most cats do not like him, but in Montana, there is a cat named Blazer who will let him lick the earwax from its ears. He can categorize. All animals can.

We make categories, therefore we communicate. *Grass* is one word for something diverse. Girl, tooth, run, small, American. There is more than one way to do and be everything. But just one word for each. To change our ways of thinking about category we would have to fundamentally change language and how it functions. We would have to change our brains. I do not think the human mind is capable of functioning without categories. When I try to think of a way around it, the only thing that comes to mind is a blur of screaming.

—m—

Down a backless set of stairs to the basement of the Boston Museum of Science.

Here: a permanent exhibit. *Natural Mysteries*. Designed to teach children about order through a series of interactive games.

Carved into a wooden post:

WHAT IS CLASSIFICIATION?

One side of the post reads: GROUPING.

The second side: COMPARING.

Through glass doors, I enter the main exhibit.

I play the Mammal Skull Game.

Pick up a skull and answer these questions: *does your skull have canine teeth? Is the eye socket shaped like a nearly completed circle?*

Through a process of elimination (holding the skull against pictures on a computer screen), I separate rabbit from cat. Herbivore from carnivore. I know whose skull is whose.

In this game, the word *generally*. *Canines are generally found in carnivores.*

The implication: something, sometimes, will not fit.

Another wooden post: WHO CLASSIFIES?

Who classified these? (A line of butterflies.)

Answer: scientists.

Who classified these? (A spoon, knife, fork.)

Answer: families.

Who classified these? (Wrenches in decreasing size.)

Answer: mechanics.

Who classified these? (Colored beads.)

Answer: artisans.

I am sad for the scientists who cannot string beads. For the artisans who cannot use wrenches. For the mechanics who cannot be lepidopterists. For the families who eat with their hands.

If there is no silverware, is there no family?

The next game: *Tree in a row.* I am to match actual leaves to pictures of leaves labeled: *elm, oak, maple.* To me, it seems as though none of the leaves match the pictures. I am forced to ignore individual differences. I am forced to seek the salient trait, the one that defines. I am taught to un-see specificity and nuance in favor of the collective. This is human. Part of our mythology. The success of our species. To sacrifice the self for the greater good.

The next game: *Make your own museum.*

At my feet, a wild jumble of materials, stored in a wooden box. Eight mini chalkboards nailed to the wall. In front of each chalkboard, a small plastic, transparent box. In each box, the materials of exhibits, displayed and named by the children who made them:

(Four pieces of obsidian.) "Museum of shiny dark rocks"

(Gold coins, plastic pink pompoms, jacks.) "Birthday Girl"

(Plastic seals, plastic whale, and a pink cloth rose.) "I Like Sea Creatures"

The rose seems to me to represent "Like" in the title.

(Walnut, shell, rock, eraser.) "Museum of Orange Things"

To me they all look brown.

(A small wooden bowling pin.) Title: "I (heart) Mike Vogel. Tori was here."

I see this as an exhibit of hope. On Friday night, Mike will see Tori at the bowling alley. Black balls thunder down wooden lanes. Three of his fingers crook tight. He is stunned by her straight, shining hair. He wants to touch her, but, lacking courage, he laughs too loud when her ball gutters.

From this exhibit, I see that children understand the flexibility of classification. They know to impose a set of qualifications, to make choices that include and omit.

I come to another set of glass doors and walk into a room lined with drawers. Inside the drawers: butterflies, moths, skulls, shells, eggs, mollusks, coral, beads, nuts, turtle shells. There is nothing sadder than an empty turtle shell. I read that a nineteenth-century woman donated the items in this room. Yes, I think. This room has a Victorian sense of artifact and order. Orientalized fetishism. I decide what these artifacts have in common is the mind and temperament of their owner. I can see no other connection between them.

I leave the room and read about the Seri Indians, skilled fishermen who have dwelled on the Northwestern coast of Mexico for two thousand years. A mainstay of Seri diets: green sea turtles. Scientific name: *Chelonia mydas*. The Seris classify turtles with ten different names. *Moonsi* turtles, are larger, meatier, than *quiquii* fatty turtles. *Cooyam* is the migratory phase of young turtles that travel up the coast in schools. Hunters know to watch for them in spring. And so on. A classification system based on what the Seri must know in order to eat. Their system is compared to the scientific classification of turtles created by biologists.

We classify based on need. On a visit to a museum it may be helpful to know the difference between a green sea turtle and a leatherback turtle, but if dinner depends on turtles it is important to know the difference between a *moonsi* and *quiquii*.

I stand still, at the exit, thinking, in front of a set of glass doors.

Suddenly, the exhibit is overtaken by a large group of school children streaming away from their chaperones. Screaming *eeewwwww* and *disgusting* and *gross*. I had forgotten. I was walking through *Natural*

127

Mysteries, trying to experience it as a child, without having childlike reactions. I had forgotten to be grossed out.

A young boy, six or seven, distraught, leads his mother by the hand from the room of butterflies, moths, empty turtle shells. As they pass me, the boy says to his mother, "If you don't want to look at any more dead stuff, follow me," and tugs her toward the exit. I look at his mother. We smile in the way adults do when a child says something wise, and I realize what everything in the nineteenth-century glassed room has in common, what the whole exhibit has in common, its overarching principle of categorization: Everything in the exhibit is dead. The boy knows it, but I did not.

Once something is dead, stuffed, etherized, it stops changing. It is taken out of time. In this way, it is falsified. In this way, it is no longer itself. A white fox and a white rabbit have more in common, lifeless, immobile. But something is always lost. Lost.

How to classify the living? How to classify people?

Humans are not so predictable or easily controlled.

We are erratic. Inconsistent.

We classify each other with every glance and thought. By color, shape, size, texture. Language, nation, race, class, sexuality, gender, age, religion, region. Our language, how we communicate, is categorical. And the only thing we have to talk about language with is language.

How human. How absurd.

—⚏—

1614. The first recorded interracial marriage in North America between Pocahontas and John Rolfe. By the time of the American Revolution, between 60,000 and 120,000 people of mixed heritage lived in the colonies. President Thomas Jefferson begged Americans to consider "let[ting] our settlements and [Indians'] meet and blend together, to intermix, and become one people." Patrick Henry proposed that intermarriage between whites and Indians be encouraged through the use of tax incentives and cash stipends.

1601, Virginia required that any white woman who bore a mulatto baby pay a fine or face indentured servitude: five years for herself, thirty years for her child. 1661, Virginia prohibited interracial marriage, and made it punishable with a fine of ten thousand pounds of tobacco. In Maryland, a white woman who married a Negro slave had to serve her husband's owner for the rest of her married life.

By 1717, Maryland's state legislature made cohabitation between any person of African descent and any white person unlawful. Between 1850 and 1860, the mulatto slave population increased by sixty-seven percent; in contrast, the black slave population increased by only twenty percent. The "one-drop rule"—the concept that even a single drop of African blood rendered a person black—took hold.

By the 1950s, almost half of the states extended miscegenation laws to unions between whites and any non-white person, or as phrased by the state of Arizona in the case of *Estate of Monks*, Caucasians were: "Prohibited from marrying a negro or any descendant of a negro, a Mongolian or an Indian, a Malay or a Hindu, or any descendents of any of them. . . ."

1958: Reverend Dr. Martin Luther King, Jr. said, "When any society says that I cannot marry a certain person, that society has cut off a segment of my freedom." Miscegenation laws not only made marriages void, they made children born of such unions illegitimate, took inheritance rights from spouses and death benefits from heirs.

Then, a case went to the Supreme Court. *Loving vs. Virginia.*

The plaintiffs, Mildred Loving (née Mildred Delores Jeter, a woman of African and Rappahannock Native American descent) and Richard Perry Loving (a white man) were residents of the Commonwealth of Virginia, and had been friends since their respective ages of eleven and seventeen. They married in 1958 in the District of Columbia, having left Virginia to evade miscegenation laws. The morning of July 11, 1958, five weeks after their marriage, the Lovings were awakened by the county sheriff and two deputies. The police burst into the Loving's bedroom and shone flashlights in their eyes. By the Loving's account a threatening voice demanded, "Who is this woman you're sleeping with?" Mrs. Loving answered, "I'm his wife," and pointed to the marriage certificate hanging on the bedroom wall. The sheriff responded, "That's no good here."

Mr. Loving spent a night in jail and his wife several more. The couple pleaded guilty to violating Virginia law. Under a plea bargain, their one-year prison sentences were suspended on the condition they leave Virginia and not return together or at the same time for twenty-five years. The judge quoted from Johann Friedrich Blumenback's eighteenth-century interpretation of race, saying: "Almighty God created the races white, black, yellow, Malay and red, and He placed them on separate continents. And but for the interference with His arrangement there would be no cause for such marriages. The fact that He separated the races shows that He did not intend for the races to mix." The Lovings paid court fees of $36.29 each, moved to Washington and had three children. They returned home occasionally, but never together. In 1963, Mildred wrote to Attorney General Robert F. Kennedy and asked for help. He referred her to the American Civil Liberties Union and the Lovings began a class action suit in the U.S. District Court for the Eastern District of Virginia. But the court upheld the constitutionality of anti-miscegenation laws and affirmed the criminal convictions.

The case went federal. Four years later, in 1967, the Supreme Court ruled in favor of the Lovings and struck down the final set of segregation laws in sixteen states.

In 2000, Alabama became the last state to remove miscegenation laws from its books.

—∞—

To my mother and me, the two great love stories of our Irish family are my grandmother and grandfather and John and Jim. John and Jim—steadfast love from 1974 to 2007, when John died in his sleep curled around Jim in the bed they shared for thirty-two years.

The first time we went out to see John and Jim, who lived in San Francisco, I was four. I don't remember walking in on them kissing passionately in the kitchen, but my mother says I did, then ran to her, crying. She thought I'd burned myself on the stove. She stood up and screeched, "What is it?"

"They're kissing," I wailed.

She winced, took me by the shoulders. Shook me gently. "It's nothing to get upset about. It's just true love. Now be a real woman and stop your weeping."

Another time, I remember walking along the wharf, the five of us, in San Francisco. I remember John and Jim holding hands. My mother and father holding hands. People staring. I remember John and Jim dropping hands. My mother and father dropping hands. Even if my mother and father had not dropped hands, I remember thinking my being there, between them, showed what they were to each other. Living, breathing evidence.

I remember the danger. The eyes like arrows. The taboo. Of John and Jim and my mother and father. The four of them, different from most people because of whom and how they loved. One couple, a love of sameness; one, a love of difference. A male nurse and a male hair-dresser. An Indian and an Irishwoman. The politics of love. Both loves, ostracized. Both loves, legislated.

Sexuality is not a choice. Skin is not a choice. Being visible is a choice. The four of them stood up, came out, no matter how alone that decision made them. It was simple: to them, there was no other choice.

There is a picture of the four of them scrunched together on John and Jim's couch. I must have taken it as a child since no one else was there and the angle on the photograph is low, as if shot a few feet off the ground. When I look at the photograph, I see a family, made, created, brave.

—⁂—

Are you your mother's child or your father's? Whose child are you? Lines drawn. Tendencies noticed, features claimed. The question seems to define with starkness, weigh heavier, when each parent symbolizes, in their entirety, a culture, language, religion, skin color, way of being. Irish-Catholic, Sindhi-Hindu. Whose child are you?

Once, in a graduate class on race and identity, someone asked me why I didn't just say I was Indian. She asked me with a challenge in her voice. As if it was her right to question how I define myself. She asked me as if she thought I was trying to get away from Brownness by say-ing I was Indian *and* Irish. As if a person could not be two things at once.

I said, "Well, to not say I'm Irish is to deny my own mother. And I could never do that. To my mother or myself. How can someone deny their own mother?" She looked shocked, as if it had never occurred to her that way.

To hear someone say

that any two people should not be together feels to me like a direct attack. Like war. Like the deepest of insults.

Once, I had a lover who said we were too different, that love was too hard if two people didn't come from the same culture.

I felt as if my family had been dismembered.

To me, the point of love is to overcome difference. Nothing is too hard for love. Not threats, not a lifetime of alienation, not money, not religion, not skin, not ruined reputation, not illness, not gigantic corporations with a long reach, not famine, genocide, poverty, government, not the power of one's raising. Nothing is too hard for love. Nothing.

In my family, difference was a way of life. A constant negotiation of respect, ignorance, new understanding. There was society, and there was our family. Public space, private space. Family was resistance. What was not accepted by society was real and lived by me and mine. Love, the great border crosser. No passport required.

There is no such thing as too different. There is only an unwillingness to love enough.

COUNTRY IS

December 2003. At the immigration desk at Indira Gandhi International Airport, the officer tries to separate my husband from my father and me. "We are together," we say in unison. The male officer hears but does not understand. Not a language barrier, but a barrier of idea. Finally, a female officer who has brought him a cup of tea leans down and whispers. "Oh," he says, "One family. Okay." He picks up his stamp.

Whump, whump, whump. Pause. Rustle. Pause. Whump, whump. The immigration song.

The smell of Delhi at five AM. Diesel, jasmine, woodsmoke. *Mouli* and *agarbati* and cloves and rubber and feces (bovine, canine, human, goat, bat). Horns and bells and muezzins and radios. Motors. The city productive, festive, in dawn's cool respite.

We take a cab. Drive five minutes then stop, strangled in traffic. The driver turns off the car and headlights. Says to me, *"Tumhara pati issuperstrah hai."* Your husband is a superstar. My husband's earrings, his bearing. He is an actor, recognized. My father laughs. My husband is pleased. He likes a nation that appreciates performance. But the honking at intersections confuses him. He has never before heard horns blared as warning, not aggression. The horn, on Indian roads, as necessary and courteous as a turn signal. Polite, informative communication. *Awaaz do.*

I feel Hindi stirring in my gut. For now, I wear it like an ill-fitting suit. It takes five days for the language to return. Slowly, at first, I say words I do not remember knowing. They appear suddenly in my mouth, when

137

I need them. After a month, I am comfortable enough to flirt with the language. But only the old women laugh at my jokes.

The dawn air, thick with human sounds, lacks mechanical hum. No bulldozers or cranes. All motors, headlights, off. I lean out the open window and watch *chai-wallahs* dipping ladles into silver vats, pouring tea in tall glasses. I hear an axe chopping wood, concrete sifting, corn grinding, bamboo lashing into scaffolding. A man in a blue checked *lungi* rolls dosas on a rock. The tips of *bidis* glow small and hot. Above the crooked flyover to our left hangs a massive billboard: NO ONE CAN MAKE YOU FEEL INFERIOR WITHOUT YOUR CONSENT.

We drive a few yards and pass two young girls and three women washing their hair at the side of road. Fully dressed, with jewelry. Lathered up. White soap on hair hanging in long ponytails down their backs. Further along the road, we stop again. The engines cut. I see a child. She looks about six years old. She is barefoot. Ragged. Hair in clumps. Skirt and blouse in tatters. Soot and dirt from the exhaust of incessant cars cover her limbs. She lives with her family on a median strip. Four feet wide and twenty feet long. A median strip in the middle of a New Delhi road.

The child is holding a stick. Two empty bottles of Dasani water, Coca Cola Company, hang at either end. What trickles down—what is retrieved from the garbage. People have what they find, what they make. People have each other. I watch the child playing with the toy that is only partially a toy. Her stick and two Dasani bottles. She can help collect water.

It is six AM. The child is awake, the shapes of three sleeping bodies around her. On the median strip, a short line of laundry. Children's clothes: tiny pants, tiny shirt, tiny skirt. Neatly hung over a line of wire stretched between two highway signs.

Someone is keeping house on the median strip. Making a tidy home. Those tiny clothes. Washed and hung up to dry.

A woman driving a motorbike with a sari guard, two children in neat school uniforms stacked behind her on the seat, honks at a Tata Sumo

SUV with darkened windows. To rest, in traffic, she puts a foot down on the median strip. The children on the back of the motorbike look at the child on the median strip.

The traffic inches forward.

In the shadow of the flyover, two men stand in the bed of a parked truck. The back of the truck loaded with red clay bricks stacked like freestanding walls. The men stand near the lowered tailgate on a flat pile of bricks. They playfully wrestle and fight. The bigger man grabs the smaller man around the waist, from behind. The bricks rise around them. The bigger man lifts his arms till they wrap around the smaller man's chest, then rocks him back and forth in a rough, teasing fashion. Their bodies smashed against each other. The bigger man holds the smaller man still. For just a moment. A moment of bodies pressed tight, flesh-to-flesh. In that one moment of stillness, I see it. They are lovers. Flirting and touching in public. A moment taken, boldly, in the name of love. Traffic stops inching, horns stop honking, ladles stop dipping, cigarettes stop glowing. For just a moment. Their love so real, so brave, it halts time. Then the bigger man drops his arms and the smaller man takes one step away and they return to the light performance, the jostling, joking wrestling, of two men without the weight of love. The bricks rise red and clay and silent around them. They stand next to each other and look out at the traffic, falling into the same stance. Hands on hips.

—⚉—

Sometimes when I ask my father how to say something in Hindi or Sindhi he says, "I forget." I am exasperated, bewildered. "But I've been here longer," he says. "It'll come back to me later and I'll tell you then." The phone rings at 2:30 in the morning. When I first open my eyes, I think it is India, time difference causing a late night call. But it is my father, from just across the East River, supplying the word.

My father's first Thanksgiving in America, he dressed up as a pilgrim. Donned a longhaired blond wig and carried a fake plastic rifle. Wore a big buckle belt and tights over a *kurta*. My mother said he kept wandering away from the turkey (which he dutifully ate bits of even though he was vegetarian) to look at himself in the mirror and laugh.

Once in my thirties I cleaned out my father's closets and lined the hallway with bags of Goodwill clothing. My father, whisking along in chappals, balancing a cup of tea on a tray, one-handed, saw the bags and stopped. Took a sip of tea, "Looks like JFK in 1971. Everyone entering the country with their lives in trash bags." Steam fogged his glasses, momentarily. He went, with his easy grace, down the hallway.

Whenever my family moved within the United States, we stuffed our lives into trash bags.

"We are Sindhi," my father said. "We move."

Now, when I pass garbage lining New York City streets, I think of Punjabis in JFK. I think that I will keep my life small enough to fit in a trash bag.

We are Sindhi. We move.

Sometimes I would wake up in the middle of the night and find my father, cross-legged on the living room floor, reading the *New England Journal of Medicine*, sipping tea. I would sit down next to him and ask, "How could you leave? How could you not go back?" To me, all that family, all that homeland, was irresistible. I wanted to know if he had abandoned them or if they had abandoned him. For some reason, I thought the difference was important. "How could you leave? How could you leave all that?" I asked, again and again. He patiently glanced up at me, kept reading. The only thing that stopped me was when he'd say, "Because I wanted to have you."

—⚏—

My husband, Holter, keeps a large American flag hanging above his desk in our living room. Over the blue square and fifty white stars hangs a cow skull he collected at the slaughter pit on his uncle's ranch. To get a cow to the slaughter pit is no easy task. We hauled one, once, he and I,

140

three miles. Tied her poor stiff legs with chains. Attached the chains to the four-wheeler. Dragged her, all 800 rigor-mortised pounds, to the pit.

Holter's uncle tells a story about Holter as a child. He went to Montana—his mother's place of birth and raising—from Baltimore. He was four. They drove a dirt road with cows, mountains, grass, on either side. They saw an American flag waving above a fencepost. Holter said to his uncle, with surprise and indignation, "Hey, that's *our* flag."

I was told this story as we walked out of a bar in north central Montana. I still had a beer in my hand; before reaching the door, I set it on a table. Holter's uncle said, "You don't have to do that. You can bring it outside and drink it in the truck. It's not really America," he said, and smiled.

I laughed, "That's what we say about New York."

Until I was twenty-three, I sang the "Star-Spangled Banner" this way: *and the rockets red glare; the mums bursting in air.* Mums. As a child, I knew that mums and marigolds were of the same family. My mother raised both in the backyard. Marigolds—the flower of India that rains down in grief, celebration, honor. I thought mums were an American take on marigolds. Mums made sense to me in a nationalist song. I envisioned mums bursting in air, along with banging, happy *phatakas*. I loved singing that line, loved the pictures it gave me. Raining mums, raining marigolds. I never paid attention to the meaning of the other lines. I sang them just to be singing along. But I felt close to both India and America when I sang: *and the rockets red glare, the mums bursting in air.*

It was a moment of shock, understanding, fear, when I was twenty-three years old standing in Baltimore's Camden Yards at an Orioles game, and I heard, for the first time, the true words to the song. Forty thousand voices singing it at once. *The bombs bursting in air.* Bombs. An entire stadium with their hands on their hearts singing about bombs. How protective the mind can be. I had converted bombs to mums; I had created a meaning specifically for myself. I had misheard for twenty-three years.

That is a long time to mishear.

Later, the whole stadium shouted out "O," as in *O, say does that star-spangled banner yet wave,* but they claimed the "O" in a forceful, celebratory shout. O for Orioles. They had taken the song and made it into something of their own, too.

As a child, driving in Michigan's U.P., Upper Peninsula, I thought it was Michigan's Uttar Pradesh, U.P. I pronounced Ramada Inn as Rama-da, thinking it was a chain owned by a Hindu father.

Once my father told me a story of a Korean restaurant in Bombay that no Sindhis would go to. It was called *Hanga ma*. Which translates in Sindhi as: *I have to crap.*

When I was a teenager, I wanted braces. That gleam of metal, exotic trips to the orthodontist, interesting little rubber bands. I wanted that rite of passage. It seemed so American. I asked my father if I needed them. "Smile," he said, and leaned over to stare at my teeth. "They're going to grow in okay. The bottom row will be slightly slightly crooked. But it is not worth the price. You'll be fine. No braces. No problem," he said, and patted my head. He was free of the American ideal of perfect, shining teeth. Teeth that were just okay were more than enough. Anything else was unnecessary, wasteful.

The American flag, post-9/11, and for approximately two years afterward, became protection for those who could be perceived as terrorists. I remember the fear for my tribe, family, friends. The hushed conversations. We were uneasy.

I made my father put American flags in his car window, house window, office window, after 9/11. He did so, happy, patriotic, filled with a cold anger at terrorists.

He always cringed when I criticized America. When he defended America, he was defending his decision of migration, of citizenship. To speak or act against America was to cut at his choices. He had not been born an American. He had worked and decided to become one, because he believed in the ideals of the country, because he had me, an American child. He would laugh nervously when I ranted about Reagan or Bush. It didn't matter to him what the president said; he was the president, voted in, and should therefore be afforded respect. I'd say, "But a good citizen questions, to make things better." "Little American," he'd say, and shake his head. He had known another reality.

He kept his Indian sensibilities, ways of living, thinking, in big and small ways. He stayed vegetarian, took his shoes off at every door, wore a *sagara*, would not eat till he'd had his morning bath and prayer. He had a special pair of tongs just for *papadum*, holding them over the gas flame of the stove, flipping the lentil discs, front side, back side, till they lost their opaque sheen and fluffed and blackened at the edges. He developed a method for souring Colombo yoghurt till it tasted almost handmade.

I used to consider my father free of America's guilt. No slavery, no Watergate, no bombing of coal workers in Matewan. He was free of the history of the place he left (because he was not there) and free of the history of the place he'd come to (because he was new to it). He was in-between histories. Sometimes I thought that meant freedom from responsibility and grievous wrongs. Sometimes I thought a new citizen must take on the sins of its new country, as well as its blessings.

My mother always said, "The Irish are the Blacks of Europe. Our family didn't get here until the 1890s. And we stayed poor and stinking in Hell's Kitchen. There's no blood on our hands." This cannot possibly be true (with family working for Tammany Hall) but the mythology is interesting—the ways we all absolve ourselves.

My mother didn't believe in unconditional love. "You've got to earn it," she'd say. "You don't get something for nothing in this world." She felt this way about government, too. A government needed to earn a people's love, just as a person needed to be a responsible citizen for their country. She believed in history and learning from its lessons. But she didn't dwell on her own past. "What's past is past," she'd say, when it came to herself.

It was always important to my father that I could potentially become president of the United States. He would remind me of this at least once a month. But I never believed him. When Barack Obama, the son of a Kenyan immigrant and a white woman from Kansas became the 44th president, I called my parents. My father took a breath, said, "You see, Nee-Nee. I made a good decision. I came to the right country." My mother said, "I never thought. . . ." Then started to cry. The next day, after reading about Prop 8, she called back to say, "What is this country coming to."

The potato brought my great-grandparents to the States. Partition brought my father. When I thought about the history of Ireland, of India, those privations and wars, the blood shed and languages lost, when I thought of the course of history, certainly, without the British, neither of my parents would be in America, and I would not exist. This

144

was the land of possibility. Not just of money and opportunity, but also of two different people, from two different places, coming together to create another, a third.

On 17th Street in New York City, there is a U.S. Mailbox tagged with graffiti: I LOVE ROHIT in white spray paint. I don't know if it was written by a *desi* person or maybe just to a *desi* person. But it seems an important milestone. We are now as mundane, as American, as graffiti on government property. We are loved, our names shouted across bridges and sidewalks and subways and mailboxes. We are here.

—∞—

My mother and grandfather always told stories of where they were when Man landed on the moon. I asked my father once, "When they landed on the moon, where were you?" "India," he said. "Where did you watch it?" I asked. My father said, "There was no such things as televisions." "Oh," I said, and realized he meant in India, then. "Did you listen to it on the radio?" "Yes," he said. But I could tell he did not remember. An American landing on the moon must not have seemed important to him. America then, to my father, was just as far away, just as unknown, as the moon.

In 1986, my mother brought home the Indian National anthem, "*Jana Gana Mana*," on a record from the library. It was the month after the Dot Busters, a hate group targeting Hindus, killed an Indian doctor in New Jersey and a week after they burned down the house of an Indian doctor on Long Island.

I memorized the anthem phonetically, not understanding every word, but pronouncing each carefully. It came to me suddenly that the melody of "*Jana Gana Mana*," sounded similar to "This Land Is Your Land." If I sang one song then the other, I felt nervous and tilted, unbalanced as a scale with rocks on one side and nothing on the other. So I blended the two and made them one song:

145

Jana gana mana adhinayaka jaya he
This land is your land
Bharata bhagya Vidhata
This land is my land
Panjaba Sindh Gujarata Maratha
From California to the New York Islands

I sang the word *Sindh* with more pride than the others. Mapped out of one country and into another. A living ghost in the Indian anthem since 1947. Something is always lost.

—๑๑—

I believe in potato salad and the sudden beauty of fireworks. That expectant lag between sound and color. I love the ones that sputter and fail. When my husband barbeques on the Fourth of July, he reads old newspapers (the headlines about Iraq, Afghanistan, Darfur, mountaintop removal) before he wads them up and feeds them to the coals.

My cousins Naresh and Rajan, on July 4, 1977. They came from Calcutta to live with my parents, grandfather, and me for nine months. The picture was taken in the backyard of the house where my mother grew up in Hicksville, Long Island.

146

I see my cousins with water guns, playing American gangster, with a little Shashi Kapoor sass to their hips.

On July 5, we went to Williamsburg, Virginia. My cousins stood in the stockades and my father snapped their picture.

My Aunt Gagi taught me to wear a sari, to fold and tuck the pleats, to check the length of the petticoat, to hide the safety pin in the *paloo* so no one would

see it. We ironed her saris foot by foot, folding the hot squares of fabric into a smooth pile.

She gave me the sari she wore when she walked alone with my uncle for the first time. "My love sari," she said. "It will bring you luck." My aunt, my uncle, good pleats, arranged by their mothers.

While I was at college my mother created Indian Feast Day for her ninth-grade students. She likes her students to don the clothing of the country they study. "Walk a mile in a man's shoes and you'll know how he feels," she says, raising a finger so they know it is a lesson.

For Indian Feast Day, her students ate mutter paneer cooked in the Home Ec room, the recipe flashing on a neon blue computer screen above the rows of white wholesale stoves. The lone Pakistani girl donated the paneer. Her mother purchased it at the Hicksville Patel Brothers and would not accept reimbursement.

Wielding spatulas, the thin boys wore my father's *kurtas*, the big boys wore my uncle's *sherwanis*. My mother found my aunt's love sari wrapped in a pillowcase in my closet. She gave it to a pale blonde, green-eyed girl who spilled milk on the *choli*. "Mrs. Vaswani," the girl said, "I've stained the costume."

—⚏—

I write this section from Kentucky. I am teaching here for six months. I am Sindhi. I move.

I am alone and have bought a plant so I will have something to care for. A Guzmania. It cost six dollars. Maroon, spiky bloom. Waxy petals. The bloom hunkers in the center of leaves that arc and droop over the sides of a terra cotta pot. On a plastic card stuck in the soil it says Guzmania must have water between its leaves at all times. It pools there, between the leaves, like webbing between fingers. I move the plant back and forth from the windowsill to the table, chasing sunlight.

I buy the makings for pickled beets and onions. Something I do in the spring and summer with my father. The Mason jars look scientific, mouth-watering, on top of the fridge. It will be hard to wait three days for the beets to fully pickle. I crave salt and vinegar. The crunch of blanched vegetables.

I pickle two jars of beets and onions, the way my aunts and grand-mother and father pickle. I feel emotional when pickling. For the first jar, I am full of joy, thinking of my family. For the second, I grieve. For my family.

The bells from St. Francis church on Bardstown Road toll the noon hour and I think of my mother. Feel the backs of my half Irish-Catholic knees curtsy before sliding into a wooden pew. I boil the beets. Baby them in my one small pot. Submerse them with a wooden spoon. They are ready when they slide off an unserrated knife. I save the juice, from the pot, smelling of steel and dirt, for vegetable stock. I save the greens to sauté with butter and salt. I hold one beet, uncut, in each hand. Like young violet breasts. Then I slice the beets. The rings of a sliced beet—like small trees.

The beet has an indomitable identity of color. It stays with you. Even if you eat only two or three slices of beet, you will see its blood in your stool. It is the most resilient of vegetables. Through stomach acid and bile, feces, and blood, it retains itself. I always think, "This is it, I am done for, I am bleeding to death from the inside," when I look into the watery depths of the toilet.

But it is just the beet stating itself.

I drop sliced beets into Mason jars and pour in vinegar. I spoon in salt, peppercorns, thinly sliced raw onion. I mark the two jars: Grief and Joy.

Once I can eat the beets, I will see if they taste different or the same.

148

My fingers are stained with the blood of beets. I see that I have not yet typed a "q" or "x."

Now I have. Now all the keys on my keyboard are violet.

I set the jars of pickled beets on the windowsill in the kitchen, next to the Guzmania. The light falls across them. The maroon bloom, the same color as the jarred beets. The white paint of the window frame and sill. The pale, afternoon light. The sunny cold of early spring blows across the jars.

My father is in Calcutta now, in my aunt and uncle's apartment. My cousin Avi is getting married today. And yesterday was Priti's, his fiancée's, mehndi and *sangeet*. My uncle Chatru sent me an e-mail saying, "Daddy is here safe and eating a lot."

That is what my father does in Calcutta. He eats his past. Relives it, bite by bite. My Aunt Renu's *gaajar ka pani*; he will spoon into his mouth. Crunch down on a *papad*, and say, "Perfect." My Aunt Uma's and Aunt Dolly's stuffed *paratha*, my Aunt Chitra's *Sindhi kadhi* and fried potatoes, my Aunt Gagi's *loli*, which her cook and friend, Lily, makes the way Gagi did before she died. An endless stream of women bearing food. The tastes of my father's past. His Sindhi will return, prodigal, to his tongue. It will be sweet, mellifluous. Lily will cover her head when the muezzin cries.

It is strange that in Kentucky I am homesick for India instead of New York. My homesickness wanders, immigrant. It is Sindhi. It moves.

149

Through the window, I see the mother and child who live next door. They are barbequing. It smells like new flowers and charred meat.

This is true: the grieving beets tasted saltier than the joyful ones.

I am alone. My country hangs, framed, above the gas stove. My country: a photograph of my parents. I look at it through the glasses my father wears in the photograph. I look at it, feeling the white hairs on my head, increasing each day, forming the same streak as the one in my mother's dark hair.

In a Dublin museum, a butterfly. Orange wings, rimmed in black. White circles at wingtips.

Tagged: *A South American butterfly collected for the Natural History Museum by Sir Roger Casement circa 1911.*

Roger Casement. Born 1 September 1864, County Dublin, to a Catholic mother and Ulster Protestant father. Hanged for treason on 3 August 1916 at Pentonville Prison, London. His corpse, the broken neck, thrown in quicklime.

His crime: at the beginning of World War I, seeking German assistance to end British rule in Ireland. The German government, reluctant; Irish prisoners of war, unrecruitable. The one shipment of weapons he acquired sank off the coast of Ireland. The Germans loaned no army officers to lead the Irish rising planned for Easter 1916.

My mother always says: "The Irish never ask for what isn't offered."

Casement returned to Ireland on Good Friday, 1916, in a German submarine, and was put ashore near Tralee, County Kerry. Of that moment, he later wrote of the skylarks, the dawn, the primroses and wild violets, the sounding surf.

Wet, he was arrested and hauled to the Tower of London. On 29 June 1916, he was sentenced to death.

His sense of humor: defiant. A vigorous participant in the Gaelic Revival, he championed Irish language and culture, both squashed under British rule. Among his papers: "an acerbic note from his bank asking him to please not correspond in Irish."

George Bernard Shaw felt Casement's defense should be that he was not English and therefore could not be tried for treason against England. It was a matter of words.

Language, Casement's weapon. His report on the Belgian Congo, published as an official government document, detailed daily life in work camps—roughly 900,00 square miles. Camps where natives were starved, flayed, raped, maimed, worked to death. Murdered.

He did not describe the act of looking; he described what he saw. People in pain. Bodies unclothed, ripped. Horror speaking for itself in unadorned language. An aesthetic, a style, that disassembled empires.

He died a Catholic, having converted, in his bed in the Tower of London. In the 1970s it was reported that his ghost made frequent appearances in Calabar, Nigeria, where he had been a consul at the beginning of his involvement with British imperialism.

A line from the Nigerian report: "The apparition was always said to be of a kindly nature."

Post-mortem. The British government published his personal journals, known as "the Black Diaries." An attempt to slander a dead Irish hero. In Casement's diaries: "erotic encounters are reduced to a few descriptive phrases of beautiful eyes, large cocks, and sexual acts." He included penis measurements in sexual shorthand.

The Irish reacted to Casement just as the English wanted them to.

151

An Irish martyr, stained by sexuality. Abhorred for his aesthetics. Abhorred for how he loved what he found beautiful.

Perhaps, naked, Casement heard more truth than as a uniformed official of imperialism. He stripped: artifice, power. It does not surprise me that he was an insomniac. Or, that, amidst atrocity, he sought pleasure. Gave and received it. It does not surprise me that he had two diaries. One public, one personal.

We are left with his words and the effects of those words: progressive, controversial. We are left with the butterfly.

After the Congo, he throttled empire in South America. Of Putumayo, he wrote: "I said to [a] man that under the . . . regime I feared the entire Indian population would be gone in ten years and he answered, 'I give it six.'"

It was within this environment of genocide and rainforest that Casement caught the butterfly, now flattened in Dublin's Natural History Museum.

It was as he sloshed, knowingly, from the German submarine toward death, that the beauty of skylarks and wild violets touched him.

Does this say something about Roger Casement, specifically? Or does it speak to the nature of beauty and atrocity? Aesthetics and politics?

Yes, beauty is subjective. But universally painful, I think. It comes from pain; it causes pain. A butterfly, alive, dead: painful.

Beauty comes from juxtaposition.

If the goiter were not there, would the woman be as beautiful? A goiter of that size is felt, experienced. My father took this picture in Nepal. In the mountains, due to a lack of salt, a person can become iodine deficient. My father took this picture because the woman was next

152

to the fruit. The size and shape of the apples showed the size of the goiter, comparatively. I did not know any of this when I first saw the picture. My father was silent as he handed it to me. I looked at the photograph. I saw the woman more beautiful because of the goiter.

Yehuda Amichai wrote:

> Sometimes pus
> Sometimes a poem.
> Something always bursts out.
> And always pain.

Beauty, like pain, is universal. Beauty and the recognition of it is not a luxury. The beauty of usefulness. The usefulness of beauty.

Even starving, alone, beaten, there is the beautiful. In the voice of a child, in a shaft of light, in a flower bending in the wind. It is there. It is defiant. It stands up, beautiful.

In New York City, at Second Avenue and 11th Street is the Settlement School of Music. Outside, on the wall of the building, a mural, painted by students. The Twin Towers, yellow and tall. Beneath the Towers, these words, scrawled in a childish hand:

> *This will be our response to violence: to make music more intensely.*
> *More beautifully. More devotedly than ever before.*
>
> Leonard Bernstein

Beauty arrests the observer. A statement is made: don't look away. See this. Appreciate. Remember.

Beauty *is* utilitarian. Beauty is political.

—⁂—

I did not officially exist until the year 2000.

The first U.S. census in 1790, supervised by Thomas Jefferson, placed people in one of three categories: free white male, free white female, and other persons. Seventy years later, the government added categories, such as Mulatto and Chinese. The 1890 census added further distinctions of White, Black, Mulatto, Quadroon, Octoroon, Chinese, Japanese, and Indian. In 1900, Booker T. Washington said, "The white blood counts for nothing. The person is a Negro every time." By 1910, the Census Bureau eliminated the terms mulatto, quadroon, and octoroon; it was assumed that three-quarters of all blacks in the United States were racially mixed anyway. Anyone with African ancestry would henceforth be counted as black. The 1910 census also asked people about their mother tongue, hoping to tally the number of Jewish immigrants through Yiddish.

From 1970 forward, the census required people to choose one of the following categories: White, Black, Asian/Pacific Islander, American Indian/Eskimo/Aleut, or Other.

For most of my life, I marked "Other" on all official forms. That sentence of directive: "Check ONLY one" turned my stomach. I refused to pick and wrote a long list of ethnicities on the "Other" line. I felt like an alien. Indefinable, unknowable. Sometimes I checked every box, as I did during the pre-SATs. I was scared my score would be nullified or my mother would flog me, but it was something I needed to do for my individual well-being.

Sometimes when I said "we," I meant my family. Sometimes I meant Americans. Sometimes South Asians. Sometimes Sindhis. Sometimes Irish-Catholics. Sometimes Biracials. And so on. A wandering, itinerant We. Shifting and changing depending upon where I am and who I am with. It is not disloyal or opportunistic. It is a reflection of my parts.

On the 1990 census, almost ten million people marked their race as "Other;" most were Latinos unwilling to identify themselves as White, Black, or Indian. Americans using the write-in blank after "Other," self-identified nearly three hundred races, six hundred Native American tribes, seventy Hispanic groups, and seventy-five different combinations of multiracial ancestry.

154

When I filled out the census in 2000, I wept. I couldn't get my hands to stop shaking. In my lifetime, I had gone from marking "Other" to the inclusive, simple "Check all boxes that apply." I checked and checked and wrote THANK YOU FOR CHANGING THE CENSUS at the top of my form.

I called my multiracial friends, a hefty crowd of varying mixtures. A group of people who had been invisible for nearly the entire governmental history of the United States. We were suddenly visible, legitimate, acknowledged, counted—and it was beautiful. The 2000 census offered six racial categories (including, for the first time, Asian Indian), giving the possibility of sixty-three combinations of racial identity. My family, my people, rejoiced.

The 2010 National Census will actively edit the responses of same-sex couples. Though same-sex couples can now legally marry in five states, the census will classify all legally married same-sex partners as "unmarried." According to Census Bureau definitions, a "family" consists of two or more people related by birth, adoption, or marriage.

On the 2010 national census, in an LGBT marriage or relationship, one person will get counted as a single parent. The other parent will not exist.

—∿—

January 2005. We are Sindhis. A roving tribal refugee argumentative easy-going card-playing dancing singing driven passionate wild resourceful whiskey-swilling ingenious misunderstood landless hard-working open-minded generous ambitious pluralistic people. We converge upon the newly opened Pizza Hut in Hyderabad, India. Four of us born in Hyderabad, Sindh, now Pakistan. One born in Hong Kong. One born in Calcutta. One on Long Island, to an Irish-Catholic woman. We have not seen each other in eight years.

The Pizza Hut is a family-style restaurant. White Formica clean and bright. Waiters and waitresses stand in parallel lines at either side of the door. Outside the rickshaws honk furiously. A fisherwoman walks by in a yellow sari. She tosses a pale green cabbage, catches it after two steps, tosses it again.

The waiter arrives in a spotless red smock and says, next year, he is going to college in Houston. Everyone on the floor speaks English. Customers, waiters, waitresses.

My uncle Chatru despises melted cheese, finds the concept mysterious and disgusting. "Eh, young man," he says to the waiter, "Bring me the garlic bread, without cheese." He orders and scolds simultaneously. I fear the waiter may cry. He is unaccustomed to the complaints of the general public. "See," my aunt Popri says to my father, "Chatru eats whatever he wants. No attention to diabetes and sugars."

In thirty-two years my uncle Chatru and I have spent 107 days together. Going east, we are one ocean, five seas, one gulf, and 3,248 rivers apart. I have counted the blue lines in the atlas. In my family, numbers console. We know how ordinary it is to vanish.

Because it is Monday my aunt Chitra is not eating meat. She looks at me and says, "One into two?" I nod. We get a veggie pizza to split. The waiter brings Chatru his chicken soup. He spoons the broth miserably, says to me, "Eh, NiNi, where is the chicken?" He shakes his head, sadly, and calls the waiter over. "Look," he says, and dips his spoon in the broth. "Do you see chicken?" The waiter tries to take the soup away, "Sir, I am very sorry," but my uncle stops him. He does not want new soup. He does not want more chicken. He just wants the waiter to see the absurdity of a chicken soup with no chicken, the absurdity of a Pizza Hut in Hyderabad and young men in red smocks.

Sachu, the neighbor's daughter who has joined us, rants about American politics, taking large bites of garlic bread. The irony escapes her. "You Americans and your weak stomachs," she says, looking at my father and me, "You all think India is dirty. Whenever my cousins from Japan come to visit, they are so finicky and they always get sick." My father and I eat silently. I want to point out to her that her cousins are Japanese, not American, and that I am not the one with toilet paper

156

in my purse. But my father and I stay silent, the NRIs (Non-Resident Indians) who take the same jabs from everyone, whether spoken or unspoken, knowing it is true, knowing we have made someplace else our home and will return there eventually. India makes us American the way America makes us Indian.

Chatru sticks up for me in his unobtrusive way. He puts a small jalapeño on my plate, "Eh, NiNi, the smallest chile gives the hottest taste." He pats his pockets. "Sachu," he says, "I forgot my wallet. You're paying, *henna?*" She puts on Bollywood dim-witted yokel eyes and cups an ear, "*Kyaa, kyaa, Angrezi kyaa hai? Hindi bolo, ji, Hindi bolo.*" We all laugh. My father drums the Formica tabletop with his fingers and the heel of his palm, tabla style. Tha, tha thicka tha.

A bell hangs in the middle of the foyer near the front door. It looks like an old temple bell. Solid knocker hanging down; little piece of rope. Whenever someone exits the Pizza Hut, they ring the bell. It tolls, and, Pavlovian, the waiters and waitresses chorus THANK YOU all together, and the rest of the restaurant joins in.

Every time the bell rings, Chatru rolls his eyes to the ceiling and says, "*Hai Ram.*" My uncle, at age seventy-six, has more defiance than the teenagers in the restaurant. He looks around the room, heavily. His gaze settles on me. "She'd come home at 5:18," he says, and I know he is speaking of my aunt, my father's sister. She has been dead eleven years.

"I would come home at 5:21. We would wash and dress and take a stroll. We would catch the ten *baja* bus to the Club and dance till midnight. Every Saturday." "You remember exactly what time she came home?" I ask. He nods, "We had been married three months. She would wait for me. She said those three minutes before I got home at 5:21 were always the loneliest. Sometimes I made her wait an extra minute. So she would kiss me more when I came through the door." He chuckles. Everyone in my Indian family reminisces about their first months of marriage, the sweetness of the early days, the way Americans reminisce about first dates.

A family leaves the Pizza Hut and rings the temple bell on their way

157

out. The waiters and waitresses chorus THANK YOU with big American gusto, along with half the people eating in the restaurant.

"*Hai Ram,*" Chatru says.

He closes his eyes. I cannot tell if he is sleeping or remembering.

Gautam drapes his arm around Chitra and says, "I met her in December 1962. And she's still my favorite girl." "My coconut," Chitra says. "Hard outside, soft inside," and squishes Gautam's cheeks together.

Chatru opens his eyes again. "Once," he says to me, "when she was a girl, she fainted and fell off the train platform. No one saw her fall. The train pulled away from the platform. Because she had passed out, she didn't move. That saved her life. The train workers recognized her because of your grandfather and lifted her off the tracks. She had not a scratch. Once a cab in Calcutta hit her. Nothing happened. She was perfectly fine. Once she was hit by a motorbike and broke her arm. All those times, she could have died. But she didn't. We had time together."

Another family leaves the Pizza Hut, rings the bell on the way out. THANK YOU, the waiters, the waitresses, my family, everyone's family, choruses.

Chatru says, "*Hai Ram,*" looks at me. "She was so weak as a girl that when she carried tea in a cup, everyone covered their ears. We went to the same Sindhi temple in Hyderabad as children. We did not know each other then but I must have seen her with ribbons in her pigtails. Maybe

158

we even sat next to each other." He sighs, looks at me, and says, "How that woman suffered before she died." He passes his hands across his face as if to wipe away the memory of her pain.

The next day, everybody goes shopping and Chatru drives me around Lake Hussain Sagar to the Salar Jung Museum, a place my father loved as a child.

43,000 art objects; 9,000 manuscripts; 47,000 printed books. Rooms of armor and jewels and turbans and ivory and jade. Chandeliers, decanters, embroidery. Mughal plates that change color when touched with poisoned food. Noor Jahan's daggers. Aurangzeb's sword. Chinese fans. Persian carpets. Waterford crystal. A diamond encrusted hearse. The Veiled Rebecca. Mephistopheles and Margaretta carved from a single block of wood.

Chatru and I time our visit to witness the noon ringing of the British Cook & Kelvey clock. Since I was a child, my father has told me stories of this clock.

It is 11:45. Chatru waves his wrist, taps his watch. "Come, come," he says. "Hurry or we will miss the moment."

The clock lives in a small room filled to bursting with human beings from 11:30 till 12:05 every day. We squeeze our way to seats at the front of the room. There is a sign on the wall: CAPACITY 100 PERSONS.

I am surprised by the clock's smallness. It is protected from the public by a velvet rope. My uncle beams at me and says, "It has been ticking time, unabated, for the past 150 years."

At the right hand side of the clock, a bearded blacksmith in a red cap and apron hammers out the seconds on an anvil. In the middle of a clock, a small brass bell hangs from a wooden tower. At the left side of the clock: a closed white door.

The crowd hums with anticipation. My uncle looks around and says, "About 130 people. Give or take." He reaches into his pocket for a hanky, then wipes his brow. In the room, there is an overwhelming sense of humanity. It feels as if we are breathing each other's breath instead of real air.

159

At 11:50, the ceiling fans switch on and begin to circle. People jockey for a good position, insulting the tall, lifting up toddlers. Mothers breastfeed babies to keep them quiet. Chatru has a mild coughing fit and the woman next to him digs in her purse and produces a peppermint.

At 11:58, silence descends upon the room and shivers, expectant. My uncle and I strain forward. I realize I am holding my breath. We all are. The woodcutter brings his hammer down on the anvil. 130 pairs of eyes focus intently on the clock.

The small white door swings open and a white-bearded wooden man in a red nightshirt trundles out. He brings a stick down upon the tiny bell. His hinged mechanical shoulder moves in stilted chops. The bell tolls, melodious. Twelve strikes, the most possible. The old man slides backward and disappears. The white door swings shut.

A moment of silence: sheer and quivering. Then applause. A swell of delighted voices.

The wonder, the novelty, of the other.

WHAT HANDS ARE THESE?

November 1994. We tucked the bottoms of our skirts in our waistbands and went barefoot into the peanut fields. The silver hoops in our nostrils tapped against our cheeks. A crack of yellow light split the grey land and sky.

Rudra showed me how to pinch the peanuts at their slender waists. She mimed a squat—thighs wide, knees flexed—and pushed the corners of my *dupatta* into my skirt so it shaded my face but did not tangle in my arms. My hair hung to my hip in a braid. I crouched, mimicking her. She shoved my braid into my blouse. It itched down my back. Her hands ploughed like shovels through the dirt.

The sun rose hot, and she stood, barrel-chested, breasts flat behind the neat darts of her green *choli*. She squinted at me in the new desert light. Her face, brutal. Cheeks of subsistence. No lies or pleasantries on her forehead. She stared at my relentless neck. I took my hands from the dirt.

"Are you poor?" she asked. "No," I said. "Skinny," she said, using the colloquial Rajasthani, *tartia*, scrawny girl—a word I was familiar with. She grabbed my arm and held it against her own: lean. I said, *Amreeka mai*, "In America, it is possible to be poor and fat, or rich and skinny." I did not say "the States." I used the mythic: America. I said, "People often eat less in America to be skinny, to look skinny. Men and women both." She did not believe me. "You are poor," she said.

My hands convinced her. She grabbed them and turned them over. She rubbed my palms. *"Tum kaam nahin karti ho?"* You do no work? She shoved my hands back at me. "I work," I said, "I serve food at a restaurant.

163

I rip tickets at a movie theater. I read and write. I think. I am a student." She clucked her tongue against the roof of her mouth, called to the women, "See her baby-hands!" They came across the field from all directions, silver doughnuts on their ankles, glinting. "How old are you?" Rudra asked. I said, *"Unnees,"* nineteen, and she pushed my *dupatta* off my head, grabbed my chin, tugged my eyelids, pulled my foot until I lifted it, an obedient horse. When she slapped my soft sole, I asked how old she was. She rose up, flicked her fingernails against my teeth. To me, she looked forty in the face. Sixty in the back, with an osteoporotic slouch. "How old?" I asked again. She flashed a spread hand, four times. *"Bees?"* I asked. Twenty? and she wagged her head. She asked, "What work does your husband do?" I said, "I don't have a husband." Her laughter came: radical, complex. The women gathered close, razzing: "There must be something wrong with this girl. Old Maid, she is an Old Maid." "I work," I said again. "It's just a different kind of work." "Thinking is not work," Rudra said. "Digging for peanuts is work. Fucking your husband is work." The women laughed. She pushed me. "Let's see you work," she said, and pushed me. "Work."

I turned my back on them and shoved my hands in the dirt. I dug and dug. I harvested. I do not remember being hot or thirsty. I remember the motion of my hands, the hatchet pain in my back, my ossified knees, rigid bladder. I felt muscles I did not know I had. I pawed at the dirt. It smelled like a drawer of silverware and goat manure. I groped for peanuts, pulling them out of the ground, my mother's favorite aphorism running through my head: *Idle hands are the devil's work.* Rudra taunted me. "Old Maid. Baby Hands. Baby Feet." She manipulated me around the field with her voice. I dug even when she rested.

Digging to my left was a pregnant woman named Sanjula who looked about thirty-five. She was the most beautiful among us. Eighteen, with three children. Straight, thick eyebrows. Tea-brown curly hair. Watchful lips. She was the one who took me to the edge of the field. I only knew the Sindhi word for piss and I did not know where to go to do it. Sanjula took me to a dip between the field and the dirt track. We squatted. She said I should work slower or the sun would make me stop. I said, "No, I am fine." I asked her, "How long?" indicating her swollen stomach and she answered with a scale of time I did not understand. Finally, she pointed to the sky and knocked on the ground seven times which I took to mean seven months. I forgot the length of my braid. It hung between my legs and I pissed on the end of it. It dried instantly. The sky, hot blue.

In the fields, Rudra came to us. She said, "Just four," tucked her thumb against her palm, her fingers pointing up. The women bent and took four peanuts from the ground. Crunched them slowly with their back teeth. Buried the shells. I copied them. When we were done, Rudra said, "Have one more each," and it was a gift. "This is money, Old Maid," she said, rattling the peanuts in her hand. "Don't eat unless I say so." I nodded.

The sun blared directly overhead. "This way, this way," the women said. We walked across the fields to a hut I had not noticed, tiny, of the same dirt as the surrounding desert. No border between peanut field and desert. They seeped into each other. We went inside the hut and lowered our *dupattas*, shook the dust from our hair. The walls of the hut, lined with sacks: lentils, corn, peanuts. It was dark, therefore cool. A rounded doorway, no door, no windows. Through the doorway, I saw the sky like an upturned blue bowl, the brown fields spilled beneath it.

Someone handed round two cold *chappatis*. We tore them into twelfths. Rudra pulled my glasses off my face and tried them on, kept a finger on the nosepiece. She removed them, handed them to Sanjula, who gave them back to me, and combed her hair with her fingers. "Where is your family?" she asked. "Calcutta," I said, simplifying matters. I picked up an empty tin pot and tried to balance it on my head. Rudra snatched it from me and balanced it on her own head. "What do the women there do?" Sanjula asked. I told her one of my aunts was a bookkeeper. "Number-counter," I rephrased. "My other aunt is a psychologist." I said the word in English then tried to explain. "A mind doctor," I said, "a doctor of thinking and feeling." "She has soft hands?" Rudra asked, and tossed the pot in the air. She caught it; it rang against her palms. "Yes," I said, "but nicer than mine. Painted nails. Gold rings. She removes the hair on her fingers." "What does number auntie look like?" she asked. "Like me, lighter-skinned," I said. "Prettier. Not skinny." "Ah, rich," Sanjula said. She stood and stretched her back. "Yes," I said.

Rudra asked me something about American women I could not understand. She stood and rocked her hips, made motions with her hands that ended in a punching of her left fist into her right palm. Everyone was quiet, watching me. "Yes," I said, "American women fuck." "Do American women fuck their husbands?" Sanjula stood next to Rudra and looked down at me. "Sometimes," I said. " Sometimes just with someone they like. And not every woman has a husband." "Our husbands are assholes," Rudra said. "They don't do things. Like this," she said, and pulled her hands through Sanjula's hair, following the strands over breasts, ribs, belly. Leisurely, they stood like lovers who had known each other as children. We all sat on the ground, eating morsels of cold *chappati*. We watched them. "Like that," Rudra said and looked at me. "Do they do it like that in Amreeka?" "Yes," I said. "Sometimes." She hung her arms around Sanjula's neck. "It's her baby," Sanjula said, stroking her belly. We all laughed. "Food is done," Rudra said. We had swallows of water from the tin pot.

We went outside, the air limpid and wavy with heat. More dirt, more peanuts, more white spears of sun. We kept our heads covered and down. The dirt warm, underfoot. I dug more peanuts than anyone else. I tracked my progress, compared it to Rudra's, kept up with her, surpassed her. I wanted to ease the workload. I did not want to be called lazy. I felt broken when still. Standing hurt more than bending, as though bending was what my body knew best how to do. When we took another break, we stayed in the fields, too tired to walk to the cool of the hut. Rudra said we could eat two more peanuts. I cradled mine. Pocked, tender food in my hand. We buried the shells, and the women surrounded me. They stroked my fingers and I stroked theirs. Our hands chapped, heavy with dirt. We held our palms together. They looked the same, felt different. My hands, dry, fingers cracked, black with embedded dirt. "Still soft, soft," the women said. "It takes a lifetime to make hands," Rudra said, and shook hers at me. We stood under the sharp sun with our skirts pulled up.

166

Rudra's hands were hard. Not scratchy. Firm with a polished armor: tortoise. On the inside of her forearm, running along her veins, a verse from the *Ramayana* was tattooed in homemade blue ink. I looked at the forearms of the other women. Many of them had the same verse, in the same ink, in the same handwriting. The "huh," curled like a snail. "The doctor," they said, "he can write. He comes sometimes." They had memorized the verse and spoke it to me. I took Rudra's arm and read her tattoo, sounded out the individual letters: *Huh, aii. Ruh, aah, muh. Hai Ram.* I said, "Together, the letters make a word." I drew Hindi in their hard hands and thought of Helen Keller. Language written on the body. Language felt and remembered. I spelled into their palms. It was an entertaining trick. We were hungry.

When the sun looked to be at two o'clock, we finished the last field. We left the peanuts loose on the dirt, to dry. We would return at the end of the week to pick and sack them. We stepped into our plastic flip-flops and headed toward the dirt track.

On the walk back to the village, I took my cigarettes from under my bra strap. We smoked some of my *bidis,* soggy, salted with my sweat, and I distributed my precious pack of Marlboro Reds. I taught the women how to blow smoke rings, and how to say *motherfucker* in English. Rudra taught me to walk with the tin pot on my head. She said I would work in the pea fields next. She said they had other work to do and would leave me with the pea women. My back adjusted to uprightness. I kept the pot on my head for fifty steps. The women herded me to the center of the group. I looked at the flat, dark land. I looked at the sky. I looked at my feet. We heard a truck coming from a long way off. We covered our heads to keep out the dust. The truck bounced past us, then stopped. The driver stuck his head from the window, shouted, "Get in." The women shouted, "No room." He drove away, then stopped again and stuck his head out the window. Shouted, "Plenty of it." We climbed into the back of the truck, crammed with white tanks of diesel. We slid into the small spaces between the tanks. The bumps, dust, painful. We got knocked around and looked at each other and laughed. Rudra stood up and we held her legs, wrapped our hands around her calves. She lifted a few tanks, stacked them so they would not topple. After a while, the women banged on the sides of the truck. It slowed and we jumped out.

We passed through the village on the way to the pea fields. I saw the other American, female students. Some bathing children; sifting lentils. There were no males in sight over the age of ten. I was the only student assigned to outdoor labor. I preferred it that way. It seemed fair that because I looked like the village women, I should live like them, too.

Rudra said to call me Old Maid so the pea women did. She told them to make sure the children *uskee Calcuttay kay hath milao,* "meet her Calcutta hands." She equated my soft hands with Calcutta, not America.

During my first hour of planting peas, some men came from the village to watch. One of them hit me across the face with the back of his hand for planting the peas in too shallow a ditch. I felt four of his knuckles under my eye. I was so surprised I sat on the ground. He pulled up my pea plants. He did not damage them even though he ripped them from the dirt viciously. I kneeled on the ground and screamed. "Pig, is this how you treat your mother? Your sister?" My voice, dry, cracked. He came at me with his fists. I covered my head with my arms. The sun hot on my spine. When he stopped beating me, I punched him in the knees. The other men came in a rush and dragged him away from me. The women stood in their furrows and watched. The men shouted. I stood and turned my back on them. I bent and replanted one seedling. Someone grabbed me. Dragged me by my braid up the furrow, over the well-planted peas. My blood fast in my fingertips. I dug my heels in the dirt. He let go. I lay on the ground, then sat up, stared, my mouth hanging open. The men flocked together. The pain in my back from digging was more profound than the pain of a beating. I did not care about the men. I was hungry. I looked at the peas. I was ashamed of the ruined food. Five plants gone. Five plants crushed by my dragged body. I watched the woman next to me. I stood up, mimicked her planting, asked her to check my work. "It's good," she said.

A pair of hands with work to do, a pair of feet with a furrow to follow. My hands, the dirt, the drape of my *dupatta,* sun, peas, other women.

The privacy of my furrow. I looked at my hands, pinching the slim green necks of plants.

When they tired of watching us work, the men wandered to their broken tractor and pushed it away. We waited until they were obscured by a hump of desert and then we stretched our arms behind our backs and tucked our skirts into our waistbands. "This way, this way," the women said. As we walked, we slapped the dirt from our hands and knees. We smoked *bidis* behind a haystack. I showed the pea women my smoke rings. We punched our fists through them as they widened and hung above us in the air. After sharing a few cigarettes, we went back to our furrows. I thought about my twelfth of *chappati* and seven peanuts with pitted shells. The children came to the field. They lined up and I held out my hands. They stepped forward one by one and stroked my dirty, soft palms. Some of the children laughed. Some were confused. The sun was hard and bright and then it darkened and I looked up and saw a cloud of locusts moving across the sky. The women began singing to the children. A song about a crow who stole the Queen's gold anklet. My arms and back were firm. There were rows of peas I had planted in sturdy lines behind me. I held one soft hand with the other.

At the end of the day, the peanut pickers came for me, traveling in a group with Rudra at the center. They looked over the pea plants with approval and took me to the main courtyard of the village to pick lice from the schoolchildren's hair. The children who did not go to school had been deloused in the middle of the day when the sun was high. "It is the schoolchildren who bring lice to the village," Rudra said. "Eight of them. Two of them girls, sisters." "These are the only schoolchildren?" I asked. Rudra said, "Yes, sometimes these children go to school."

Picking lice was light work. We made a circle. Between every child, a woman. We plucked the lice and nits. In the middle of our circle, a small tin pail of grey, soapy water. There was one comb, green plastic, a man's comb, the tines straight and close together. We passed the comb around and scraped it through the water to keep it clean. In the children with black hair, it was easier to see the white eggs, like glued poppy seeds.

169

Children with reddish-brown hair, like mine and Sanjula's, were more difficult to delouse. Most of the lice were at the back of the head, above and behind the ears. The women turned delousing into a lesson of numbers. Approximately twelve eggs per head. We counted out loud, all together, the children shouting: E*k, do, teen, chaar....* With the help of the schoolchildren we added together the amount of lice in the heads of boys and the heads of girls. With the help of the schoolchildren, we reached one hundred and ten. I had never counted above fifty so I learned new numbers, too. One of the girls had adult lice. We parted her hair and watched them, little beige grains, racing up and down her scalp. They were too fast to count so we made up a song. "Run run run, run off Bhusa's head." The sun spread oval against the pea fields. We sang and counted to the beat of our grooming. I liked the nimble motions it required of my hands. I asked Rudra if she would take me to see the school, seven kilometres away. She said, "When the work is finished." I never saw the school. I kept a journal for the nine months I lived in India as a student. I wrote nothing for the weeks I stayed in the village. There was too much work and I had forgotten a pen.

The sun went flat on the horizon. We sat in a row against the side of a mud hut, the walls so dry they thinned against our weight. Sand drizzled down our backs. We looked out at the brown fields and sewed sacks that we would later fill with peanuts. It was the only time my left-handedness became visible. I had not written anything more than a few Hindi letters in the women's palms. No one noticed I smoked with my left hand; it was the hand for dirty things, anyway. All other tasks were two-handed. I thought of the extravagance of one-handed tasks. Write, turn a page, hold a phone, click a mouse. At first, Rudra tried to make me sew with my right hand, thinking I was being my usual, stupid self. "No, no," I told her, "I'm left-handed," using the Sindhi word, the only one I knew, but she did not understand. "I use this hand," I said, waving my left. "The other one doesn't work for me." Someone said "*maur*" and I looked up and saw a peacock streaking across the field, blue neck extended, feathers spread and shimmying with a glint like water. "Male," Rudra said. "They have good color." Then she said something I did not understand. Everyone laughed. She simplified her language for me. "Same place," she said, and patted Sanjula's belly. "Girl, boy," she ticked the two words off her finger, "both come from the same place. Only different once they're outside the stomach." Someone said, "Hey, Rudra. Even your husband came from there." "Not him," she said, "He came from rooster shit." She looked over at me, checked my work. "Stupid baby," she said. I fumbled with my sack. She snatched it from me and showed me how to stitch the seam closed in a straight, quick line.

We sat sewing for what seemed a long time. The light lingered. I developed a long thin blister on my left thumb and index finger. It was wondrous to sit. I looked up from my work, startled, when a man's voice said my name. It was Jatan. I simplified again and told the women, "This is my brother." They teased him. He was wearing a jacket and tie; he had a walking stick. He smiled good-naturedly, looked at his watch, said we were late. "For what," I asked. He said he had finagled me an invitation to the headman's house. The women tilted their heads at English. I told Rudra I wanted to go but I did not want to stop sewing. She asked me why I wanted to see the men. I said I wanted to know what they did, what it was like for them. "They don't do anything," she said, and dismissed me with a shove. It was hard to stand up. My knees buckled. My back hunched. The women laughed.

Jatan walked fast as we traipsed along the terraced edge of the pea fields. He was not my brother, but he was like a brother. I asked him what he had been doing all day. We spoke English. It felt like cheating. Or dreaming. He griped about carrying sacks of lentils and said the rest of the time they had sat on the broken tractor and talked. "Very interesting ideas," he said. "The headman has excellent business sense. They'll do well for themselves in the new market." "For how long," I asked, "Did you carry the bags of lentils?" "What does it matter," he answered, "Don't you want to discuss the peanut market?" "No," I said, "tell me how long you carried the sacks." He said, "The peanut is a drought-resistant crop." "No shit," I said. "Tell me how long you carried the sacks." "You're black as Kali," he said. "How long?" I demanded. "About an hour," he shrugged. "Did you eat anything?" I asked. "Some women came," he said. "We had

171

a nice meal of *dal* and rice and milk." I grabbed his hands. Soft. They looked white against mine. I displayed my palms: dry, blistered, blackened. I spread my fingers like the tail of a male peacock. "Why don't you wash," Jatan said. "We're going to dinner," and he swung his walking stick so it thwacked the tops of the pea plants. "Don't fuck with the fucking peas," I said. "That's the fucking food you ate." "What's wrong with you?" he said. I shoved him and he stumbled, caught himself with his walking stick. He was mad. I did not care. "Why haven't you been working?" I asked. The words croaked out. He wiped his jacket where my hands had been. He said, "Why should I work when you will do it all?" I walked away from him. Swung my arms and hips. "I see you're still the same brute," he called out. "Rough little village girl." If I had turned around I would have beaten him to death with his stick. He ran to catch up but I did not forgive him for being stupid and useless.

When we got to the headman's house, five men sat watching television and drinking whiskey. The headman had electricity because after dark he tapped into the line that powered the school. A dubbed re-run of *Falcon Crest* played on the small TV. I had never before seen *Falcon Crest*. Black and white lines furrowed the screen. All the women looked purple and fuzzy; their pearls, green; hair, orange. I was shamed by the fullness of cleavage and thighs. Jatan said it was an episode from ten years ago; he could tell by the actors' hairstyles. My stomach gnawed when I saw a commercial of a mother in a pink sari handing a glass of milk to her son. The second commercial was American, undubbed. I don't remember the product but I remember the words to the jingle: *Whatever you want, whenever you want it.* I stood at the back of the room, listening to the men talk about the tractor parts and peanut markets. They spoke a mix of Hindi and English. They asked Jatan about Hollywood and snow. The men, Jatan, seemed a different species. It was like spending time with hamsters. I fiddled with my hands. I thought about peas. Tried to calculate how much I had planted. I took Jatan's whiskey and gulped all of it. The men stared at me. Jatan laughed. When *Falcon Crest* ended, I slipped out the door.

Rudra must have been watching for me. She saw me coming across the pea fields and walked to meet me. "What were they doing?" she said. "*Kuch nahin karthay hai*," I said. Nothing, and she grunted. When we got close to the cooking pit, I saw all the women and children, stacking dry cow-dung patties in front of the fire, slapping *chappatis* from palm to palm. Rudra steered me toward a vat of peanut oil used for cooking. The side of the vat marked DIESEL in English from its former life. She skimmed her finger along the lip of it and rubbed a light coat of oil into her hands. She indicated for me to do the same. The oil soaked into my knuckles. "*Sookha.*" Dry, I said. "You'll go back to thinking," she said. I nodded and covered my face with my hands. "Food is ready," she said. I breathed into the privacy, the luxury of my palms.

We cooked and ate in the dark, outside, the wind shaping the fire into orange peaks. The children ran around counting. How many women, how many boys, how many nose rings, how many pink *cholis*, how many green, how many eyes and chins and feet. Off in the distance, a peacock screamed, male or female, no one could tell. We rolled out corn *chappatis* on a round rock and ate them with *dal*. It was good.

—⚏—

The bride. *Farangi*. Foreigner. To herself.

She is testimony, evidence. She is immigrant, between homes. She is beheld. She is alone.

Katie Bradford, an hour before becoming Katie Bradford Dillehay.

173

Me: weighted. Necklace flared on collarbone. *Lehnga* of cinnabar eddying waist to foot. Lips, scarlet. *Choli* stiff with gilded stitching. Earrings hung to shoulders. *Dupatta*, eclipsing bare stomach, layering breasts. Eyes bolded in black *kajal*. Arms slung with bangles. Ankles cuffed by jan-gling *payal*. Hair threaded through the cavities of 120 gold beads.

Later, at night, the beads rolled on the taut bed as he undid my hair saying the word: *patni*, wife.

As a bride in Calcutta I bore, on my body, twenty-eight pounds of gold and silk. I walked slow, prudent. My embroidered hips, my heels (five-inch), ticked.

Every prisoner wears a uniform. Every soldier. Every official.

In white, the widows laid their hands on me, tenderly, to bless.

—∞—

An Indonesian saying: "Art is thought expressed through the hands."

Mehndi: by the hands, for the hands. Cheap, impermanent beauty. It weighs nothing. In three weeks, it disappears from the flesh.

A poor bride, a rich bride, equally adorned.

When first applied, mehndi is wet, thick as clay. Squeezed from a small plastic tube with a slit at the end of it. Cool, therapeutic, on the fingers and palm. The greenish-black of mortared plants.

It is best to sleep in mehndi, to let it dry, harden, for fourteen hours. Then, awaken and flake the crusted pattern. A *darshaan* of the hands. A *darshaan* of the self. Beneath black, there is red.

The hand. Exploratory, intrepid organ. Reaching far from its trunk. Instrument of the fifth sense: touch. We touch something to know it. We make contact. In the dark, the hand knows what the eyes cannot. It eases around corners. It reaches the top shelf. It sorts, arranges, classifies.

The story, one sentence long, of the American slave, about to be sold away from her family, who cut off her hand and flung it in her master's face.

Until her bridal mehndi fades, a wife does no housework.

Woman, honor thy hands. Let them be idle, let them be tools of beauty alone, on at least this one day.

December 2003. Rukiya moved with the quickness of controlled irritation. Other people's hands meant work for her own. She whisked into the crowded lobby of my uncle's apartment building where I leaned against red pillows on the white-sheeted floor. She elbowed my aunts and cousins aside and dropped down, cross-legged, next to me. Her sari: the pink of wet azaleas, the green of tennis courts. She squeezed my wrists like unripe bananas.

175

Amisa, her daughter and assistant.

A wiry, efficient girl, thirteen years old. Ardent, lotus-shaped face and a long, black braid like an arrow pointing down, drawing the eye to the earth. Amisa sat between two silver bowls. One filled with lemon, sugar, cloves, oil; the other with ground henna, eucalyptus, and Nilgiri tea stirred to a thick paste of mehndi.

That night, my hands were the hub of Rukiya's attention. My body, her canvas. She created a geometry and I kept my fingers spread so I would not smear her patterns. Between us, a quiet intimacy. She drew the mehndi according to the shape of my hands, feet, shins, forearms. She drew fluid, spontaneous, her lips in a concentrated pleat.

On my left palm, a swirl grew into the neck of a peacock. A checker-board on the saddle of my right palm. A gate of close, straight bars. Scales, fishlike above my knuckles. Lacy ferns on the pulp of my thumbs. A squat arrow on my pinkie, indicating a flower with a center of kibbled seeds. The paisley horn of a rhinoceros on the arch of my right foot. On each toe, shafts of cilia. Above my ankles, vines sprouting. Across my left wrist, a line demarcating frontier—end of Hand, beginning of Arm. Sideways, along my left index finger—arches, like holy entrances to mosques.

Anatomy understood. Each joint and border, feted.

Between the designs, spaces. The spaces were me—my flesh, the negative realm of Rukiya's pattern. Sometimes she filled an emptiness with a dot, as she did for the head of the peacock, to make an eye so it could see. She capped the tips of my fingers with solid gobs of mehndi; I was suddenly aware of my finger pads as one extremity of self, one place where I ended and everything around me began.

All over my left hand, she drew totemic eyes with watchful pupils to protect against evil. The etymology of *left*, in English, is *sinister*. I am left-handed. Deviant. In Calcutta, I eat with my right hand and say, "Excuse my left," when reaching for *achaar*.

The last thing Rukiya drew on my body, among the wreaths and swirls of my right palm, was the letter "H," the first initial of my husband-to-be. She copied the letter from a cocktail napkin where my aunt Chitra had written it.

—m—

When I was a child in Vermont, someone gave me a paint-by-numbers set. A pair of hands, praying. It said Jesus on the box—the hands painted beige, the background, blue. Palms together, fingers skyward, like steeples. To me, they looked like hands in *namaste*, in *pranaam*. I painted from the wrist up. I painted the hands blue for Krishna. The nails I stained red. The

background I sponged black with small arcs of green. When I showed my father, he laughed and said, "*Chari chhowkri.*" Mad girl, in Sindhi.

Mehndi requires patience. Three hours work for Rukiya; three hours stillness for me, followed by at least ten hours of restricted movement. An all-consuming distraction is a wise thing to impose upon a bride. It is difficult to think philosophically while something fragile and wet is applied to twenty percent of your body.

Mehndi creates a pause, a forced calm.

I did not shift, walk, scratch, urinate. My aunt Chitra fed me, placing *tikiyañ* coated with chutney in my mouth. My cousins Archana and Bela took turns with a glass of water, holding the straw between my lips. A teenaged boy from the fourteenth floor with hair to his chin and bug-eyed sunglasses came downstairs to DJ. He played *Mundian To Bach Ke Rahi* twelve times in a row when he saw me singing along. I tried to tuck my hair behind an ear and smeared a print on my left palm. I relapsed into vigilant stillness, watching my family sing and dance, the women fanning their own wet, mehndied hands. People visited me in shifts.

We caught up on news. Who had given birth, who had moved from Dubai to Lagos, who had gotten a promotion in computers, who had died, who had returned as a ghost. My father and husband-to-be made dowry jokes. My uncle Chatru called me *guddi*, the word

pronounced so sweetly, I cried and smeared my mascara. He said, "Eh, NiNi, don't you wish you had Durga's extra hands?" I laughed so hard I cried again. My cousins cleaned my face. I was an invalid to ritual.

I leaned against the red pillows and looked at the folds of my *lehnga*, felt the weight of *kundan* around my neck. I smelled the swags of marigolds hanging at the corners of the room. They had been strung by women bony with hunger. In the old days, itinerant Sindhis—traveling for trade or as bhagats—had worn their belongings. A woman donned all her skirts at once. All her jewelry. Conveyable property. I thought about status and economic success as proudly displayed on the bodies of women. I could not help but to calculate the disgrace of abundance, the abjectness of beauty.

The cost of what I wore could have powered thirty wells in Bengal.

I was an archetype for the sake of the photographs.

Somewhere in Calcutta, there is a child named Manku. She is always in her body. There is no other way. My wedding *lehnga* could have, should have, taught her to read. If she read what I am writing now, she would wonder how she got here. She would wonder at the uselessness of could have, should have. She would wonder at the accident of birth.

In Bangkok, I once walked by a closed massage parlor. Through the window I saw a line of women, masseuses in white smocks, massaging each other's backs. I wondered if

179

Rukiya would paint her daughter's mehndi when she married. Or, perhaps she would leave her hands defiantly bare to show that on this happy occasion she had not labored.

At midnight, I extended my hands to my husband-to-be. He searched the mehndi until he found his initial. "There it is," he said gently in English, and suspended his finger above the still-wet spot.

A roar of celebration from the throat of my family.

—❦—

It is said the darker the red of your mehndi, the more your husband will love you.

Throughout the night, I doused my hands in lemon and oil, to set the mehndi and enrich its color. We were staying at the Tollygunge Club, host of the first Pan-Asian Women's Golf Tournament, and former playground of British officers. In colonial days, the club was prohibited to Indians. Now, it is prohibited to certain Indians:

I had never slept in a hotel in Calcutta before; it felt strange not to be with family. I lay awake all night, flat on my back, elbows propped, mehndied hands in air, mehndied feet dangling off the bed. I thought about my mother as she had been when I was a child. She was home now, teaching in New York.

How sensible the old ways are. Three weeks till mehndi fades. Three weeks to transition from daughter to wife.

My mother's hands: white, lean, liver-spotted in the Irish way. She never wore a wedding ring because it aggravated her arthritis. Whenever someone asked, she said, "I don't need a bauble to remind me of love."

When I turned six, she enrolled me in French for first-graders. In my memory, Madame Dupont: the jump of her white neck noosed with fake pearls as she trained me to articulate phlegm.

I enjoyed spitting, like my uncle Chandru with *paan*. My mother forbade it, even with the pits of cherries in the backyard where I zigzagged, hacking covertly, hoping to sow a forest.

When I spat out pits, I was scolded. When I spat in French, my mother heard advancement. Heard how we'd moved up in the world. *Le monde.*

In French, *être* (to be), and *avoir* (to have). Two phlegmy, irregular verbs of great importance.

When I turned seven, my mother took a part-time job in real estate to pay for a Hindi tutor. She told my father: "You come home too late to teach her; she's got to learn or she won't know who she is."

They did not see me spying. I straddled the banister, a fast horse.

She hired an engineering student, a freshman, named Deepak. Gujarati, Jain. She did not boil potatoes or kill flies in his presence. My lessons lasted two hours. Afterward we ate lunch. My mother treated Deepak as if he, too, were her child. She gave us jelly and crackers and spoke in aphorisms: "Better to be dead than powerless. And how do you get power?" She'd pause for me to say the rest of the sentence, Deepak waiting expectantly.

I would sing it: "Get an education."

Sometimes she said, "Money is power," but that she pronounced with bitterness.

From Hindi to English, *to have* and *to be* translate into each other. In Hindi: *mujhe dhukh hai*. Literally (*I have sorrow*), translates in meaning: *I am sad.* To have, to be, interchangeable.

181

In English, *to have* is a verb of ownership, acquisition.

I do not like the words *my* and *wife*, or, *my* and *husband* next to each other in a sentence. There is something conditioned, something outside of love, between that adjective, those nouns. But language is unavoidable. A trap. And so, in the *gurudwara*, my hand and the hand of my husband were tied together with blessed thread.

Something in the hand is possessed. Finders, keepers. Hands take, hands acquire. By the same token, they give. In English, the word *hand* used interchangeably with *give*. Hand it over. Hand it to me.

From the moment mehndi is applied, it begins to disappear. That is part of its beauty. Its opposition to the illusion of constancy. It pays tribute, and then it is gone.

My mother did not wear an Indian bride's traditional red, nor did she wear a Western bride's traditional white. She married my father in a purple silk sari sent air mail from Calcutta. She peeled the postage from the package and added it to her childhood stamp collection. I have it now.

—ᴍ—

I fell asleep sometime in the early morning. I know it was after five because I heard the monkeys drop from the trees to the roof of the guesthouse. I fell asleep and dreamed it was my wedding day. In the dream, each minute that passed, the mehndi on my hands faded. In the dream, I hid my bare hands, behind my back, from my aunts and cousins.

When I woke at ten ᴀᴍ, my mehndi was dry, crumbling. I went outside and rubbed my hands together under the laundry spigot where the dhobis cleaned sheets. The black shell of mehndi washed away. Underneath: my hands, dark red. Symbolic. I read them like a book. I was a woman of glyphs. I was a bride. I looked up through wisps of smog and watched a *kapasi*, yellow-eyed, perched in a kunchandana tree wound with a ratti vine. The black and red seeds of the ratti vine have two uses— rosary beads and unit weights for goldsmiths. Each ratti seed weighs 120 milligrams. Always. It is a certainty.

A sweeper-woman cleaned the path behind me. She swept my way and grinned at my hands and feet: "*Aaj tumarhi shaadi hai?*" Today is your wedding? I nodded. She clucked approvingly at the darkness of my mehndi—"La, la, la, how he loves you." She had already seen my husband-to-be. He tipped large and everyone working at the club knew this. She held up one finger, *Ek minute*, and disappeared into the trees. I kept watching the birds. Bulbul, shikra, kingfisher. The woman returned and tossed a thin garland of marigolds over my head. She called me *beti*, daughter. I thanked her and missed my mother. I watched her sweep, the yellow dirt sifting around her bare feet and the edge of her flaming blue sari. She moved away from me, up the path. I sat staring at my mehndied hands until I saw a snake, black, rippling over a rock with its whole body. We humans walk with such a small part of ourselves touching the ground. Two little slabs. I looked down at my feet and sniffed my palms. They smelled like clay, like menstruation.

At the edge of the golf course, I saw a woman jogging in saffron-colored Nikes and a sari like mint ice cream.

183

Someone yelled, "Fore!" Someone yelled, "*Dekho!*"

I went inside and woke my husband-to-be. He sat up and hunched over his knees. I laid my left mehndied hand against his back, adjacent to his tattoo, his Scottish clan crest, and used one mehndied finger to take a picture.

I told him I would not wear a wedding ring. I would not cage a single finger.

He nodded and said, "That's a good sentence. You should use it somewhere."

—⁓—

The wife. She. Not I. She.

184

That first day as a wife, she was frightened of her hands.

When she stepped from the bath, she saw herself in the mirror. Red hands and arms: shocking. Vermilion streak in scalp—the sign of a married woman. She was changed. It must be so. Her body, different. The state of bride, finished. And now, this category of wife.

It happened throughout the day. She made the bed, reached for a glass, opened a door, and saw her hands. She thought a stranger was near, or she was bleeding. Then she remembered. The hands were her own. She was a wife. Under the mehndi, her life line, scrawling down; her love line, fragmented; her head line, bisected. She rubbed her dry hands with butter.

On the second day as a wife, her mehndi was darker, deeper. She stood at the mirror and held her fingers against her naked stomach. She flapped them like the fins of a fish. How strange her hands looked holding a pen, ironing, opening the fridge. Mehndied, her hands were rendered basic, their humanity, brazen. They looked best against the nude form, against grass, soil, cupping water.

On the third day, she took the subway to Kalighat to receive the goddess' blessings. The tips of her fingers like the goat blood in Kali's preparatory pit. The goat is always male. The sacrificed male going to slaughter, the world over, for he cannot give milk or children.

It is said when Sati, Lord Shiva's wife, killed herself after her father insulted her husband, Shiva began his dance of destruction. Beneath a mauve sky, he walked the earth, grieving, carrying the corpse of his wife. Lord Vishnu sent his *chakra* to cut Sati's body to pieces. The bits of her fell in fifty-one spots throughout India. The dismembered body of a loved woman became sites of holiness. A finger of Sati fell on the land beneath the temple of Kalighat.

She thought of this as she stood before the doors of the goddess, waiting for a glimpse of the black cheeks, the burning eyes.

The doors flashed open. She looked into the face of the goddess.

She left the temple and crossed the river on a bridge of boats, upturned, held together by rusted chains. On the west side of the river, she lifted her camera and held it to her eye. Boys came and surrounded her, speaking Bengali. In their childish mouths the language was understandable. They wondered aloud where she was from, and what was attached to her eye. One boy said she must be from Bombay, far across the country. All the children agreed. She was from Bombay. She said nothing to correct them. She said nothing for there was nothing to say. She was from Bombay. They had said so. She knelt and pressed a hand in the dirt. It left a hazy print. The children knelt and pressed their hands around hers. She thought of Grauman's Theatre, the handprints of movie stars embedded in cement. Famous hands walked on by anonymous feet.

The children played with rocks and a bottlecap. She looked through her camera at the temple across the river. She watched, through the eyepiece, as the morning goat was led to slaughter, his testicles tight and jiggling. She did not take a picture.

Epilogue: January 2008. Five Years Later.

Gate G7, Newark International, nonstop flight to New Delhi.

Already, at the gate, we are out of country. Out of the United States. Everybody arguing, laughing, sighing in Hindi, Urdu, Punjabi, Gujarati, Tamil, Sindhi, Bengali, Malayalam, Telugu, Nepali. Scooping *namkeen* in neat cones of paper, *chunnis* hanging crooked across wide soft backs, long bony backs, one pink or purple or green end trailing on the floor. Babies wandering into families of strangers. Lifted up at the armpits. Auntie this, Uncle that. Tinkle of anklet, click of bangle. Sweater vests, hankies. Empty sacks of Dehra Dun rice stuffed with boxes of L'Oréal to color white hair in dark heads smoothly.

At the gate, two young hippies seeking enlightenment. Glaring at the newer crowd of laptop-toting businessmen. I prefer the businessmen to the hippies. They seem more respectful, less ignorant. As if they are (suddenly) taking India seriously. As if they will not be easily swayed by false prophets. Other than money. As if they respect the burgeoning Indian economy as a potential competitor. To view someone as a competitor is to at least acknowledge their complexities. Their realness. The businessmen react better than the hippies to the mad push of bodies at the gate. They elbow and shove and smile in vague apology to harried stewardesses. The crowd bunches, spreads, like oil on a cold *tawa*.

It is my first nonstop flight to India. No Frankfurt. No Amman. I think of New Delhi teeming at one end of the flight, New York City teeming at

187

the other. I feel the grief of leaving, joy of returning. A two-way sensation, like double-sided tape.

Arriving, departing, fills and defines a space inside me.

After eight hours in the air, I see a thin sliver of waning moon reflected in the wing of the plane. I watch *Choker Bali* on the compact TV embedded in the seat back in front of me.

A stewardess pushes a food cart. Her black hair bunned, lips scarlet. She is beautiful like a doll and moves carefully. Makes no banter. Aware of men's eyes in a guarded way. I say I am not hungry and she looks distressed. "Take some, take," she says, handing me a Hindu vegetarian meal, her expression sisterly, concerned. But I am airsick and say no. She gives me a package of *supari*, sugar and cumin, to freshen breath, aid digestion. The foil glitters. "Culinary Epilogue" stamped across its face.

After fourteen hours in the air, I look out the window and see the desert of Iran, oil fires flagging left, then right, in gusting wind. After eighteen hours, the shine of Gangamma's sleek face, stars blinking off the black tip of wing. A red line pushes the digital plane on my screen: dotted to show where we have yet to travel, solid to show where we have been.

We are at the outskirts of New Delhi.

From the air, even in darkness, I see agricultural squares of brown land: uneven, homemade. The mind of each farmer, law of water, sun, soil, hands, oxen, ploughs, made into visible shape. How different from machine rows of the Midwest, a patterned earth, lush where sprinklers fall, curved where combines turn. From the air, Delhi glows dull, steady, orange. A dim lightscape compared to the fragile twinkling of New York. The compact fluorescent bulbs and cookfires of Delhi shed a patient, durable light. The New York skyline, permanent Christmas, blinking, festive, spearing the horizon.

When the plane jolts and rolls against Indian ground, I cry and think of my father leaving India thirty-eight years ago, and the strangeness of me, returning. The journey, in reverse. I always feel I will die in India. The rule of land. It cannot be left without consequence. And so this land will one day claim me. Take me back. Keep the balance.

When the plane touches ground, all the stony, tired faces drop. People flip open their cell phones. On this end of the journey, family waits at the airport. Mothers, fathers, grandparents, sisters, neighbors, newborns. Joy, a shoving rush—an immediate shift in manners and personal space.

I feel a quiet invisibility. In India, if dressed right, no one gives me a second glance. Or tries to place me. On first glance, I fit. On first glance, anonymity. At longer than first glance, my foreign markers rise. How I walk, speak, make eye contact, laugh.

The Americans on the plane are slow to stand. Cautious. Hanging back. Now, they are foreigners. All it takes is eighteen hours. The change, via air, wrenching, deep.

Foreigner to native. Minority to majority. Suddenly, knowledge is power.

We deplane. Queue up at customs. Prepare for the official passage from country to country. It is the thirteenth of April. We left New York on the eleventh. The twelfth has disappeared, eaten by the International Date Line. Lived, perhaps, by someone else. Here, there is no moon. It is already new.

The immigration line for non-Indian citizens winds as long and lumpy as the citizen line. An equal number of Indians stand on both. We are parallel to each other, separated by passports, choices, necessity, birth. No one stands in the diplomat line but three men sit behind the desk, jawing, doing nothing.

The sound and flourish of visas, stamped. Whump whump whump. Pause as the page of the passport gets turned. Whump whump. Immigration has a rhythm. A timing of its own. We stand at the false creation of border. An open area made orderly by temporary poles and tape arranged in dog-legging aisles. We stand, tamed, one in front of the other, between the poles and tape. We wait.

To the left of immigration, a duty-free display window. A blonde mouse scoots around bottles of Johnny Walker. A tiny scrap of life running, behind glass. Beyond the immigration desks, a motionless baggage belt. Suitcases stacked, end to end, next to the belt. Electricity, money, conserved. Men with jobs, carrying bags.

I see a little child. About four. Olive-beige skin of a *desi* baby. Dark brown hair in a bowl-cut. Wobble-stomping away from her father, who struggles, each time the line moves, to drag his awkward suitcase forward. The child could be a boy except that she wears earrings. Gold studs. And so she is a girl. Intrepid and fearless. Roaming around the legs of strangers, grabbing knees for support. Her father watches, tsks once in a while, shouts her name now and then, but she won't listen; she's too bold, too willful, and anyway, there is nowhere for her to get into trouble. The child stands two-and-a-half feet tall, shorter than the poles and lines of tape. She does not see the poles. Does not know they exist. Does not know we are all in line. Suddenly, she spies a stroller. She traverses beneath, subterranean. Toddles fast and wanting. Squats down and grabs the feet of the baby in the stroller.

Let's call the child Nindatha.

The line moves. Nindatha's father roars her name then struggles with his suitcase. He moves it forward three inches, the space of one slender human being. Nindatha ignores him. Obsessed, open-mouthed, with the baby in the stroller. The baby's mother, in a black *chaddar* and gold slippers, leans on the push-bar of the stroller. Her head lolls repeatedly to the side as she falls asleep standing up. Nindatha's father settles the suitcase, roars again. Nindatha looks up, still holding the feet of the baby. Her little face, stormy. She releases the baby's feet and stands. There is not far for her to go from squat to stand. She cocks her hip and flings her small hand toward the stroller. Her white plastic bangles clack together. She stares at her father and makes one high, short, indignant sound that conveys across the wide space, *I'm doing something important. There's a baby here and I'm looking at it.* She squats back down, out of sight. The father leaves the suitcase, which topples on its side with a loud thud. He drags himself along the tape and poles, shoving and squirming into the waiting people, growling apologies, until he's in reach of Nindatha. He leans over the line of tape, bending it with his stomach, grabs Nindatha's hand, and hauls her away from the stroller. She makes no sound. They walk on either side of the tape. He hunches over to keep hold of her hand; her hand stretches high above her head to keep hold of his. They walk, the tape between them, back to the suitcase. She walks stumpy, a little slower than her capabilities, not quite obedient, but unprotesting. As soon as he releases her, she wanders away, and he does not stop her. He rights the fallen suitcase. It is clear they have these arguments, these understandings. A give and take all their own.

The line moves again. The father kicks the suitcase forward an inch or two. He looks up and sees that his wife, many people ahead of him in line, has passed through immigration. She has been stamped. She has walked between the desks to the open space on the other side. She has been cleared. She is free, over there, in India.

The child makes a determined beeline for the baby stroller. The fathers calls out to her, sweet, cajoling, "*Nindatha, Mama kay paas jaldi jao, jao, jao, abi, jaldi karo,*" (go to mommy, go, go, now, quickly). He motions wildly with his head as he grips the suitcase with both hands. The child hears him, resists, sets her mutinous chin, stamps purposeful toward the stroller, but, slowly, the word, Mama, eases down, sinks in, passes across her face. Mama, Mama. She stops, turns and smiles at her father. Squeaks. Runs through the people, under the lines of tape, her father tense with worry, craning his neck, tracking her haphazard passage. She runs and runs, and then she is free of the tape and the poles and the line of waiting people and she enters the narrow strip of space crossed only when an immigration officer says, "Next," and she runs through that strip of space, unseen, fleet, past the guards in army berets, machine guns strapped diagonally across their chests, she runs, flop-footed, between the immigration desks, no passport, no stamping, no questions, invisible, she runs and runs across the white open tiles and flings herself onto her mother's legs. Face-first. She does not put her arms out. She runs her whole body straight against her mother, who laughs, bends, and lifts Nindatha up.

191

ACKNOWLEDGMENTS

History is something that never happened written by someone who wasn't there.

—Ramón Gómez de la Serna

This book does not claim to be everyone's truth. Memory transforms; stories change with each telling. I write this book as an offering—one version of a larger narrative—as subjective as it is loyal.

Thanks to my parents for their bravery and example, for telling stories and enduring my prodding.

To trusted first readers and beloved old friends: Robin Lippincott, Sabrina Brooks, Amy Lipton.

Much gratitude to everyone at Sarabande. Thanks to the American Studies and English Departments at University of Maryland, Spalding University's brief-residency MFA in Writing Program, Knox College, and the Seward Park Center for Reading and Writing (NYPL). To John Caughey—champion, advisor, friend. Susan Leonardi and Rebecca Pope, Maud Casey, Lory Dance, Jaimy Gordon, Myron Lounsbury, Sherri Parks. Josh Woodfork who got me through and understands. Wilton, for the right words at the right time. Ranjana Varghese, John Sloan, Jason Brown, Kapil Gupta, Tara Maria, Cyn Kitchen, Jacqueline Mathey, Laura Lee, Kelly Van Zile, Cheryl LaRoche, Sena Jeter Naslund, Crystal Wilkinson, Karuna Morarji, Vinish Gupta, Jitendra Sharma and family, Mridu Mahajan, Ankit Pogula (who took the beautiful photograph on page 188), Chandra Prasad, Milica Paranosic, Carmen Kordas, Roger Bonair-Agard, Paola Prestini, Shumona Goel, Dip 2006, The House family—especially Silas for reading an early draft a lifetime ago, Jason Howard, Marianne Worthington, Kate Larken, Sylvia Lynch, Denton Loving, Aimee Zaring, Paul Hiers, and Ami Jontz.

To Elwood and Julia Kent, Nanikram and Sita Vaswani, John Crimmins and Jim Landry, Ann Clary and Jim Gordon, Hugh Davis and Janet Graham, Clans Vaswani, Jhangiani, and Dhanani, Clan Clary—especially Dick, Clan Gordon and Alan.

Most of all, to Holter, my unfailing home. First and last reader. Scarce as hen's teeth. And Lugnut, who picked us.

And to trees for these pages and everything else they give.

—⁓—

Parts of this book originally appeared in the following publications:

94 Creations, The Cimarron Review, Green Mountains Review, Motif: Writing by Ear, and *We All Live Downstream: Writing About Mountaintop Removal.*

One section of this book was awarded the American Studies Association CHASA prize. One section premiered at the Whitney Museum of American Art in New York City as "Body Maps," in collaboration with VIA, Kronos Quartet cellist Jeffrey Zeigler, and visual artist Erika Harrsch.

—⁓—

Thank you to the following works: The section on Roger Casement, beginning on page 150, quotes directly from Rebecca Solnit's invaluable *A Book of Migrations,* "The Butterfly Collector." Information on U.S. miscegenation law and the National Census gleaned from: *What Comes Naturally: Miscegenation Law and the Making of Race in America* by Peggy Pascoe, *Tell the Court I Love My Wife: Race, Marriage, and Law—An American History* by Peter Wallenstein, *Almighty God Created the Races: Christianity, Interracial Marriage, and American Law* by Fay Botham, "The American Melting Pot? Miscegenation Laws in the United States," by Barbara C. Cruz and

194

Michael J. Berson, *Virginia Hasn't Always Been for Lovers: Interracial Marriage Bans and the Case of Richard and Mildred Loving*, by Phyl Newbeck, and *Sex, Love, Race: Crossing Boundaries in North American History* edited by Martha Hodes. Information on South Asian immigration to the United States culled from *A History of Asian Americans: Strangers from a Different Shore* by Ronald Takaki, *Passages from India: Asian Indian Immigrants in North America* by Joan M. Jensen, *The Karma of Brown Folk* by Vijay Prashad, and *A Part, Yet Apart*, edited by Lavinia Dhingra Shankar and Rajini Srikanth. Information on Partition taken from *India Partitioned, Vol I and II*, edited by Mushirul Hasan, *India's Partition: Process, Strategy and Mobilization*, by Mushirul Hasan, and *Gender and Empire*, edited by Philippa Levine. Information on 1965 Indo-Pak War taken from the "Understanding Pakistan Project," and *India-Pakistan War, 1965* by Hari Ram Gupta. Statistics on cholera in Sierra Leone from archived files on CIDBIMENA, "Chad, Ethiopia, Ivory Coast, Cyprus, and Worldwide Cholera Epidemics: 1970–1971." Long Island history derived from a LIPA, *Long Island Population Survey: 2003*. Information on oral cancer from The Oral Cancer Foundation, and *Radiation Therapy Planning* (second edition), by Gunilla C. Bentel. Simon and Garfunkel lyrics from "The Boxer." I first encountered the Yehuda Amichai poem on page 153 in Amitava Kumar's essay, "Line Byline: Poetry As and Against Journalism." The story of the American slave "about to be sold away from her family, who cut off her hand and flung it in her master's face," is from Michael Neill's *Putting History to the Question*.

Holter Graham

Neela Vaswani is author of the short story collection *Where the Long Grass Bends*. Recipient of an O. Henry Prize, her fiction and nonfiction have been widely anthologized and published in journals such as *Epoch*, *Shenandoah*, and *Prairie Schooner*. She has been a visiting-writer-in-residence at Knox College, the Jimenez-Porter House, the Whitney Museum in New York City, IIIT Hyderabad, and other institutions. She has a Ph.D. in American Cultural Studies from the University of Maryland. She lives in New York and teaches at Spalding University's brief-residency MFA in Writing Program. An education activist in India and the United States, Vaswani is founder of the Storylines Project with the New York Public Library.

864007

ITEM IS ON HOLD

end of the story /

ode: 32088024014810

04/14/11 02:29PM